"KNOCK IT OFF!"

"Sorry." The reporter lowered her camera. "But you two just made the front page of the next edition."

"Well, if it's a photo you want," Jack said, not even then realizing what he was about to do, "try this." He turned Mary Jo in his arms, tilted her face toward his with a hand to her soot-covered chin, and kissed her.

Mary Jo was stunned into immobility. She barely knew the man. She didn't like public displays, and the kiss was meaningless, but it didn't feel meaningless. It felt heartstoppingly real and . . . important. It felt hot, elemental. Sexual.

It terrified her.

Before she could gather herself to shove him away, he raised his head and grinned that irresistible grin from the day before. "Yep." He winked at her.

*Winked.* She couldn't remember the last time a man had winked at her, and he'd done it twice in two days.

"I'm ready for that affair whenever you are, darlin'."

## WHAT ARE *LOVESWEPT* ROMANCES?

*They are stories of true romance and touching emotion. We believe those two very important ingredients are constants in our highly sensual and very believable stories in the LOVESWEPT line. Our goal is to give you, the reader, stories of consistently high quality that may sometimes make you laugh, sometimes make you cry, but are always fresh and creative and contain many delightful surprises within their pages.*

*Most romance fans read an enormous number of books. Those they truly love, they keep. Others may be traded with friends and soon forgotten. We hope that each LOVESWEPT romance will be a treasure—a "keeper." We will always try to publish*

## LOVE STORIES YOU'LL NEVER FORGET BY AUTHORS YOU'LL ALWAYS REMEMBER

*The Editors*

Loveswept® 844

# SPONTANEOUS COMBUSTION

## JANIS REAMS HUDSON

**BANTAM BOOKS**
*NEW YORK · TORONTO · LONDON · SYDNEY · AUCKLAND*

SPONTANEOUS COMBUSTION

*A Bantam Book / July 1997*

ISBN 0-553-44543-X

*Published simultaneously in the United States and Canada*

*Bantam Books are published by Bantam Books, a division of Bantam Dou-*
*bleday Dell Publishing Group, Inc. Its trademark, consisting of the words*
*"Bantam Books" and the portrayal of a rooster, is Registered in U.S.*
*Patent and Trademark Office and in other countries. Marca Registrada.*
*Bantam Books, 1540 Broadway, New York, New York 10036.*

PRINTED IN THE UNITED STATES OF AMERICA

OPM    0 9 8 7 6 5 4 3 2 1

# PROLOGUE

Two Oaks, Texas, wasn't the end of the earth, but there were folks who swore it was within spitting distance. With a population of 1,992, Two Oaks was a quiet town. The residents liked it that way. The only excitement anyone could recall since prohibition was lifted was that time a couple of years back when someone had sent a mail bomb to the newspaper office and blown the place up. The bomb had almost cost Two Oaks its only newspaper and the paper's publisher, but instead of a loss, the town experienced the gain of a new police chief in the former Texas Ranger who had solved the case.

Also since the bombing, Two Oaks had taken some of the money ol' Virgil Sneed left the city in his will when he died back in '57 and hired a new fire chief. Brad Conner, the former chief, had been a good enough ol' boy, but he'd been a volunteer, and the old adage of "you get what you pay for" carried more than a kernel of truth. Brad quit shortly after the bombing, so the town called one of its own stray lambs back home to do the job.

Jack Riley had grown up on his folks' dairy farm just past the edge of town, but he'd gone off to school down at the U of T, then got himself hired at the Dallas Fire Department. Did pretty good for himself down there, too, making lieutenant, then moving on into arson investigation. Learned more than a little about explosives along the way, to boot.

Jack seemed like the perfect man for the newly salaried position of fire chief of Two Oaks. Folks there didn't like feeling vulnerable, didn't like having to count on the state or the feds to take care of their problems.

Now they had themselves a gen-u-ine experienced fire chief to ramrod their volunteer fire department, and everyone breathed a little easier. Especially Jack's mama, now that she could keep a closer eye on her youngest son.

'Course, since Jack came back two years ago there hadn't been any more bombs going off to need investigating, but that was just fine. No arson, either, unless you count Mabel Ditwiler settin' her wandering husband's clothes on fire. Nobody would have cared much about that, figuring Deeter had it coming, except Deeter had been in those clothes when Mabel set the torch to them.

Since then—*then* being a year ago last spring—things had been pretty calm around town. There'd been the occasional traffic accident, although not too many since the stoplight had been installed on Main. Now folks mainly griped about having to wait for the light to turn green. But at least it slowed down those reckless teenagers.

Last summer Arliss Kelley's daughter moved back to town, which was good news. That family had sure had it rough over the years. First the son, Jeff, died in Desert Storm, and not too many years later Arliss's husband, Tom, a Texas Highway Patrolman, was killed. Tom had been standing at the side of the highway over near Lubbock issuing a traffic ticket when a drunk driver had run him down.

Arliss had been alone then, since their daughter, Mary Jo, had married Al Simpson from Oklahoma right after college and had moved to Oklahoma City. Arliss might not have liked having her only daughter live so far away, but she was sure proud of those two grandchildren Mary Jo and Al had given her. Arliss lived for calls and letters from young Andy and Heather.

But there had been more trouble for the beleaguered family. About two years ago Arliss had been awakened in the middle of the night by a phone call. Everyone knew that middle-of-the-night phone calls brought nothing but bad news, and this one was no exception. Mary Jo's husband, Al, an agent with the Oklahoma State Bureau of Investigation, had been shot and killed in the line of duty.

Another family funeral, another flag-draped coffin. Another loved one lost to duty to his fellow man.

But Arliss was content these days. Last summer Mary Jo had finally packed up Andy and Heather and moved home to Two Oaks. And high time, folks said. No properly brought up daughter of Texas had any business living in Oklahoma, and that was a fact.

So things were rolling along pretty smooth in Two Oaks.

It was a shame they wouldn't stay that way.

# ONE

On her way home from work Thursday afternoon Mary Jo Simpson totaled her car. She had a great deal of help doing it from a blue Chevy, a black Toyota, a red Dodge pickup, a sturdy utility pole, and a solid inch of ice on the street.

Mary Jo was inching her way down Main when a blue Chevy slid through the stop sign and broadsided her, knocking her Chrysler across the intersection and into the front fender of the Toyota coming from the opposite direction. The air bag exploded from the center of Mary Jo's steering wheel into her face, knocking her head forcibly back against the padded headrest.

The sting of being slapped in the face by an air bag exploding at the velocity of two hundred miles per hour was shocking and painful. And dark. For one instant, stark terror held her heart still. Her face was covered! She couldn't breathe! She couldn't see!

Immediately the bag began deflating. At the same time, Mary Jo heard another impact of metal ramming into metal and her car gave a violent jerk and shot sideways.

Mary Jo fought the air bag and cleared it from her face in time to brace herself for yet a third impact as her car was slammed sideways against the utility pole at the street corner.

Dazed, Mary Jo looked around and realized that a fourth vehicle—a pickup—had collided with the three-car-tangle and together the four vehicles had slid across the intersection until stopped by the utility pole crunched into the passenger door of Mary Jo's car.

With her heart pounding, Mary Jo was just starting to realize that she was all right when something hit the top of her car, directly over her head. She jumped and let out a startled shriek.

More thumps and thuds came from overhead, accompanied by a sharp sizzling sound, like . . .

"Oh, my God!"

Sparks of electricity were shooting off the top of her car, dancing over the other cars.

The impact of four vehicles slamming into the utility pole must have been more than the ice-coated power line could take. The line that hung high over Main Street at the intersection had snapped. Mary Jo could only assume that the loose, *live* end of the high-voltage line was . . . "—on top of my car!"

Some deeply buried instinct for survival kicked in and held Mary Jo still, scarcely breathing lest she make a wrong move and get electrocuted. She moved only to flinch involuntarily every time the downed line on the top of her car flopped and thudded and shot sparks.

Panic urged her to move, to get out. Get out now! But she couldn't. Not only was she afraid to touch the door handle, the door wouldn't have opened if she'd tried. The Chevy was buried nose-first smack against her driver's door, the utility pole against the other.

Now was a fine time to remember that she'd really wanted a four-door but had settled for a coupe.

Overhead the power line flopped again.

Mary Jo jerked. Her skin prickled as the hair on her arms stood on end.

"Ma'am? Ma'am? Are you all right?"

For one hysterical moment, Mary Jo thought the utility pole had spoken. Then she saw the man standing just beyond it, bent over and looking in through her passenger window.

"Are you hurt?" he asked.

Mary Jo swallowed. Was she? She thought hard before answering, for suddenly she wasn't sure. Maybe she had hit her head, but on what, she couldn't imagine, other than the padded headrest behind her and the air bag in her face. But why else other than a crack on the skull would the smile of a man she'd never seen before suddenly make her feel calm and safe?

"No," she called out. "I'm not hurt." *Delirious, delusional, rattled,* she thought, *but not hurt.*

With the next flop of the power line on the roof of her car, the sense of calm and safety deserted her. She flinched.

"It's all right," the man called. "Just sit tight and don't touch anything metal. The power company's on the way to cut the juice to the line. Then we'll get the other cars out of the way and spring you."

Mary Jo heard him, but her gaze was drawn to the sparks arcing past her side window like exploding rockets on the Fourth of July.

"Don't look at the sparks," the man called. "Look at me. Ma'am? Look at me."

He was right. Looking at him was a much better idea. "I'm okay," she managed. "Am I going to get fried?"

"No way." The man grinned. "As long as you're in your car and don't touch anything, you're safe as a baby."

She wanted to believe him. Desperately wanted to. But the flopping and thudding and sizzling taking place mere inches above her head mocked his assurances.

"Just sit tight," the man called.

Sit tight. If her nerves wound any tighter

they'd snap. But something about the man, his voice, his calm blue eyes, soothed her, warmed her.

Until that moment she hadn't realized she needed warming. She'd been driving with the heater on full blast, but the engine had died when the Chevy pushed her grill-first into the Toyota. The heat had been off less than two minutes, but the January cold was already seeping in. To restart the car—if it would even start—meant touching metal.

Mary Jo thought then to look around at the other cars to see if anyone was injured. As the other drivers were all staring in horrified fascination toward the roof of her car, she assumed they were all right for the moment and looked away.

"You're safe," the man said as if sensing the renewed rising of her fear. Once again his calm eyes and voice settled her nerves. "I promise."

She believed him. He was a total stranger, and for all she knew, he knew nothing about the dangers of downed power lines, but she believed him. Those eyes would not let her down.

And it was odd, but she seemed warmer, or at least less cold, when looking at him.

He was certainly nice to look at. Because he was stooped over to see into her passenger window, she couldn't be certain how tall he was but she guessed at least six feet. His hair, sun-streaked gold, but mostly the color of ripened wheat, was too short for the January breeze to mess with. His face was tanned and rugged, all planes and angles that might have appeared harsh were it not for those blue eyes and that engaging grin that made her want to grin right back.

It was while staring at that grin and finding herself indeed grinning back that she realized he wasn't a complete stranger. She had seen him around town. Unless she was sorely mistaken, he drove a red pickup and had been eyeing her for weeks. And truth be told, she'd done some eyeing back. The mere reminder had a blush heating her cheeks.

The line overhead flopped and sizzled. Mary Jo flinched.

"Don't think about it," the man outside urged.

"What else am I supposed to think about?"

"Think about having an affair."

Mary Jo stared at him a moment, stunned. Then she burst out laughing. "With you?"

"No, with Santa Claus. Of course with me." One eyebrow arched up. "Women say I'm irresistible."

"I say you're full of it."

"Is that a yes or a no?"

"I'm afraid I'll have to pass," she said, feigning sadness. "After all, I don't even know your name."

He grinned that grin again, like an ornery,

unrepentant young boy who was up to no good. "Jack. And you are . . . ?"

She laughed again. She enjoyed laughing with this man. "Mary Jo. My name is Mary Jo."

"Okay, now that we've got that out of the way, when do you want to start?"

It was a struggle to keep from laughing again. Who would have thought having a wreck, with a live electric line dancing just above one's head, could be so much fun? "Start what?" As if she didn't know.

"As if you don't know exactly what I'm talking about."

Her laughter broke free. The man was outrageous, and fun. "I'll have to check my schedule."

"Fair enough." His grin widened, then he glanced up. "Ah, here comes the cavalry."

Mary Jo followed Jack's gaze to see that the power company had arrived. Right behind them came Fire Rescue. Within moments the flow of electricity to the broken line was cut off. Mary Jo sagged with relief. An instant later, reaction set in and she started shaking like a leaf in a gale. Closing her eyes, she forced three slow, deep breaths, striving for calm that would not come. Then she opened her eyes and he was still there, the man whose eyes stilled the tremors inside her. The grin came back. His, and hers.

She reached for her key, turned it, and got nothing but the grinding sound of a car refusing to start.

A minute later the police arrived, and within moments all but two cars involved in the accident were leaving.

Through all the activity, Mary Jo watched Jack as he helped push cars until they found traction on the icy street, directed traffic around the accident site, spoke and laughed with the drivers of the other cars, the policeman, the three volunteer members of the Fire Rescue team, and two men from the café on the corner. She watched the way he moved, with long, confident strides. The way his eyes crinkled at the outer corners and deep lines formed in his cheeks when he smiled.

Watching him kept her mind off the cold. That fact alone deserved, at the very least, a headline on the front page of *The New York Times*. Mary Jo Simpson was . . . was what?

"Interested," she whispered to herself, stunned. She couldn't believe it. The last time she'd been interested in a man, in watching the way he moved, in wanting to talk to him, see him smile . . . well, the last time had been forever ago, and the man had been Al. She'd loved him, married him, had his children, and buried him. No man had sparked her interest since Al. That one did now startled her. Maybe even scared her a little.

There were only two cars left now, Mary Jo's, since it refused to start, and the car buried nose-first into her driver's door. Yet even after the tow truck hauled the other car away from her door, Mary Jo was still trapped; both that door and the one bearing the imprint of the utility pole were jammed.

Jack turned toward her again. She watched him, her heart beating just a little too fast, as he approached her side of the car. Leaning down, he asked through the window, "You doing all right?"

That silly grin spread across her face again. She just couldn't help it. "Except for being stuck in here," she called back.

"Are you warm enough?"

"For now."

"We'll have you out of there as fast as we can," he said with a wink. "Think about that affair. That'll keep you warm."

No kidding. The mere thought of having an affair scalded Mary Jo's cheeks.

It was ridiculous, of course. She wasn't the affair type. And the man named Jack wasn't serious anyway. He was only joking.

In the end it took the Jaws of Life to pry open her door and get Mary Jo out of her car. If not for the ruggedly handsome man she couldn't seem to take her eyes off of, she might not have found any enjoyment in the experience at all. But when she was finally able to get out of her car, he was there with a big, warm hand to steady her on the ice.

Then, somehow, she became separated from

him. The policeman, Charlie McCommis, took down her name, address, and phone number, and Dalton McShane, the police chief, offered her a ride home. She was too big a chicken, and too private a person, to allow herself to ask Dalton about the man named Jack.


Mary Jo may not have been able to bring herself to ask questions about Jack, but that didn't stop her from thinking about him. She was still smiling to herself more than an hour after getting home.

And really, she had no idea why she was smiling. Her car, less than a year old, was totaled; until the insurance company could arrange for a rental, she was afoot. Had the accident been more serious she could have been injured, even killed. Her children would have been orphaned and would have had to live with her mother. Yet Mary Jo was smiling, because a man she'd never met before had smiled at her.

"Mary Jo, you need to get out more," she muttered. Then she laughed out loud. Good grief, now she was talking to herself. What was happening to her?

Whatever it was, she was reluctant to let go of it. For the first time in longer than Mary Jo cared to remember, she felt alive and excited. Over a man. Which was utterly ridiculous.

"I wish I'd been there," Andy complained for the dozenth time.

Mary Jo rolled her eyes. "I'll try to give you advance notice next time I have an accident."

"Jeez Louise, the Chief of Police and everything! He even drove you home, and I wasn't even here to see it!"

Mary Jo deliberately refused to dwell on Andy's fascination with cops. He would outgrow the idea of becoming one. Please, God, he would outgrow it. He was only nine. Surely he would change his mind a dozen times over the years about what he wanted to be when he grew up. As his mother, Mary Jo was determined he would find a safe, sane occupation. One that wouldn't get him killed.

"Are you sure there wasn't any blood, not even a little?"

Heather wrinkled her nose. "Gross."

Mary Jo sighed. Gross was her six-year-old's newest favorite word.

"Are we poor now?" Heather asked.

"Yeah, Mom, are we poor since we don't have a car?"

"We're not poor. We're not rich, either. And we do have a car, or at least we will when the insurance company gets us a new one."

"Can we have a red one this time?" Andy asked.

Mary Jo smiled and ruffled his hair. "No."

Over supper Mary Jo accommodated the

kids' requests by describing the accident in as much detail as she could remember.

"A downed power line! Cool."

"It was not cool," Heather argued. "Weren't you scared, Mommy?"

"I sure was. But a nice man stayed close and made sure I was all right." And made the most outrageous proposition.

"Was he a cop?" Andy wanted to know.

"No. He was just a man." The thought made Mary Jo smile.

She tried again to tell herself she was being ridiculous, letting herself get so excited over a man, but later than night, after the kids were asleep and it was time to paint, bright color appeared on her canvas.

Startled, Mary Jo stepped back and looked. How had that happened? Where had the yellow come from?

Mary Jo had begun painting at the suggestion of a grief counselor a couple of months after Al had been killed. With Al's death, everything inside Mary Jo had turned to ice. If it hadn't been for Andy and Heather, she wasn't sure she would have survived losing the only man she'd ever loved, but the children of that love had needed her, forced her by their very existence to continue living.

But living, she had learned, did not necessarily mean living the way she was used to.

Things had changed inside Mary Jo. When she lost Al, she lost her art.

He'd been so proud of her designs, the awards she'd won. There was little on earth more satisfying to Mary Jo than working and shaping gold or silver, adding a stone here, a gem there, to create her own unique jewelry designs.

When she'd made Al's necklace, containing birthstones for her and the children, he had bragged about it for weeks. He'd been worse than a new father with his first picture of the baby. Everyone he met was forced to inspect the necklace.

Mary Jo realized that for the first time since his death two years ago, the memory of Al's pleasure over the necklace made her smile. She'd been right to move away from Oklahoma City and all its memories. Returning to Texas, and more specifically to Two Oaks, had been the right thing to do. Right for her, for Andy and Heather, and for her mother. It was a relief to smile when thinking of Al.

Now, miracle of miracles, color was appearing on her canvas.

The counselor had suggested painting as a way to express her emotions. In theory, if she could work through all the stages of grief on the canvas, eventually her art, her creativity, her ability to design award-winning jewelry, would come back to her.

So far, her painting had been black, gray, now and then purple for pain. Once a slash of deep, dark red had allowed her to vent her anger at Al for throwing himself in front of his partner when bullets were flying and getting himself killed.

Not that Mary Jo wished Zane Houston had died in Al's place. Lord knew Zane had wished it himself for months after the shooting. As partners for several years, he and Al had been closer than most brothers. But Al should have been wearing his bulletproof vest, damn him. Had he been, he would still be alive.

Dark red—the color of blood—for anger. Purple for pain. Black and gray for the emptiness she felt inside.

Now, yellow. For a sudden lightness of spirit? For a renewed interest in life?

"Come on, girl, call it what it is. Interest in a man."

Okay. She could say that, at least to herself. She was interested in—okay, *attracted to*—a stranger named Jack.


The next day at work Mary Jo was still thinking about Jack and it was starting to worry her. Her concentration was shot.

"I'm sorry, Bob," she told her boss. She'd just screwed up the inventory control sheet for the second time.

"Don't worry about it." Bob Yates, owner of the only jewelry store in Two Oaks, gave her a sympathetic smile. The gray streaks in his hair gave him a distinguished air. He had the build of an athlete gone to seed, a wife who bossed him around, and a cousin, Harry Yates, who was county sheriff.

Mary Jo had heard rumors of a troubled, hell-raising youth, but to look at him, she couldn't imagine Bob Yates getting up the energy or the nerve to cause trouble.

He patted her shoulder with a soft, manicured hand. "After that accident yesterday," he told her, "your mind's bound to wander."

"That's no excuse." Mary Jo was getting irritated with herself; her car was the farthest thing from her mind. She simply had to stop thinking about a man with calm blue eyes, had to stop remembering his smile, had to stop imagining . . . things she had no business imagining. "I'll have everything redone and finished, ready for the audit, by the time you get back from Dallas."

Bob frowned. "With this weather keeping everybody home, you ought to have plenty of time. I doubt we'll have many customers this evening or tomorrow."

There was no window in the cubbyhole that passed for the back office, but Mary Jo didn't need to look outside to know that the world as she knew it was still covered in ice. "Unfortunately," she said, "you may be right."

Bob sighed and checked through his briefcase one last time. "No use worrying about it. Business will pick back up as soon as the weather warms."

Mary Jo sincerely hoped so. She didn't see how Bob could afford to keep paying her salary if sales didn't increase soon.

"No frowning," he said. "I told you, spring is our busiest season. Wedding rings, graduation gifts. And Valentine's Day is good, too. Oh, that reminds me. That shipment of Rolex watches is due any day. If it comes in while I'm gone just put it in the safe. For whatever good that might do," he added.

"No kidding. I thought they were supposed to get that fixed this week." A fat lot of good a safe was when the only time the lock would engage was when the door was open.

Bob shook his head. "They called yesterday saying they couldn't make it until next Wednesday. Can you believe it? A jewelry store with a safe that won't lock."

"I won't tell if you don't."

Bob chuckled. "Right. Do I have everything?" He checked his briefcase again.

"You're going to your mother-in-law's," Mary Jo reminded him. "You're not supposed to be taking work."

"You sound like Karen."

Mary Jo smiled. "Just remember—it's Karen you're married to, not this store."

"Now you really sound like Karen. And if I don't get out of here right now," he added, checking the Rolex on his wrist, "we'll never make it to Dallas tonight."

Mary Jo rose from the desk and followed him down the short hall past his own office—larger, and with a window overlooking the alley—and out into the showroom.

"Oh." Bob stopped behind the glass display counter. "I'm sorry, we didn't hear anyone come in. I hope you haven't been waiting long."

The customer was a man Mary Jo recognized. Two weeks ago she'd sold him an engagement ring. She greeted him with a smile. "You came back."

The man cleared his throat. "Uh, yes."

While Mary Jo stepped up to the counter to wait on the man, Bob said good-bye, leaving to pick up his wife for their weekend trip to her mother's in Dallas. As he left, the UPS man entered with the delivery Bob had been expecting. Bob paused and turned back.

"Go," Mary Jo told her boss. "You were supposed to leave an hour ago. I'll take care of it."

After a short pause, Bob nodded, waved good-bye and left. The waiting customer told her to go ahead and take care of the delivery, since he was in no hurry.

Mary Jo opened the box and verified the contents. If she was any good at whistling, she would have let out a long, low one. Three top-of-the-line, *expensive* men's Rolex watches, each worth more than many of the cars in town. If Bob hadn't told her the other day that he had a buyer for them she would have seriously questioned his judgment in investing in this type of inventory. A Rolex wasn't the usual thing their Two Oaks customers were looking for.

Shaking her head, she signed for the shipment and carried the box back to her boss's office. There she stored it in the safe.

When she returned to the customer, he was looking decidedly uneasy. "I'm sorry you've had to wait. What can I help you with?"

After clearing his throat three times, he finally explained that his engagement was off and he needed to return the ring.

"You're sure you don't want to wait and see if the two of you can work things out?"

"Uh, well, no." He tugged at the collar of his dress shirt. "She, uh, well, she . . . found someone else."

"Oh, I'm sorry." Mary Jo offered him a smile of commiseration. He was a nice looking man in his late twenties. "I'd say it was her loss."

He blinked in surprise, then blushed. "Well, uh, thanks. Anyway, I was wondering if I could, uh, well, get my money back."

As much as Mary Jo hated to lose the sale, she sympathized with the man. Who wanted to keep a beautiful—and quite expensive—reminder of a love gone wrong?

She checked the ring to make certain the stones had not been exchanged for lesser quality—Mary Jo knew her stones—then processed the credit to his credit card account. The look of relief on his face as he left the store a few moments later told her he was glad to get the business behind him.

Only one more customer came in that afternoon. Since Mary Jo didn't want to tackle the inventory again until she had enough time to finish it, she decided to save it for tomorrow. She spent more time that afternoon than she cared to staring at the dying ficus tree in the front window. It was just about the ugliest thing she'd ever seen. But she was so used to it that she scarcely noticed it. Instead her mind wandered back to the man named Jack. She couldn't seem to get him out of her mind.

At five o'clock Mary Jo locked up the store and headed for home. She was driving her mother's car until her insurance company could arrange to replace hers. On the way home she had to buy gas, drop a suit off at the dry cleaners, then stop at the grocery store for a gallon of milk. It was unbelievable how much milk two growing children could go through.

The thought of her children reminded her of Andy's visit to the store on his way home from school that afternoon.

*His backpack.*

Only then did she remember that he'd left his backpack, filled with schoolbooks and, no doubt, his inhaler, on the file cabinet in the back office. He had other inhalers at home for his asthma, but the one he took to school was a new brand and seemed to work better than the others. She would have to go back and get it. Besides, the kid wasn't getting out of his homework merely because he couldn't remember where he'd left his books.

The lock on the rear door of the jewelry store was old and easily picked. Cold air rushed in, then a quiet *snick* as the door was softly closed. The security lights in the front showroom were no challenge, as they didn't penetrate the shadowy hallway.

Nerves made sweat gather inside leather gloves. Determination ignored the nerves. What was to be done would be done. There was no going back. No other way. And really, no harm to anyone.

The town square was nearly deserted when Mary Jo returned. Not that there had been much traffic, vehicular or pedestrian, when she'd left a short thirty minutes earlier. Everyone who had a choice was home, gathered around their respective supper tables, shielded against the cold of the January night.

Mary Jo parked in front of Two Oaks Gems. Her headlights bounced off the large plate glass window and nearly blinded her. She killed the headlights but left the engine running. All she had to do was dash in and get Andy's backpack.

As she stepped out of the car she caught the faint scent of wood smoke from someone's nearby fireplace, making her wish she was home.

Behind her a horn honked. Mary Jo glanced across the square to see Faith McShane, publisher of the *Two Oaks Weekly Register*, wave at her. Mary Jo waved back. Faith had several employees, yet she always seemed to be the last one to leave the newspaper office each night. Mary Jo wanted to tell her to knock it off, to go home early and spend more time with Dalton while she still had him.

For an instant, envy reared its ugly head. Faith had a husband to go home to at night, a man who loved her fiercely.

Mary Jo shook her head at herself and turned toward the jewelry store. Having been married, as Faith was, to a cop, Mary Jo couldn't envy the woman. Never again would she get involved with a man with a dangerous job. The risks were simply unacceptable.

A sudden need to see her children, to pull them close and keep them safe, seized Mary Jo. She unlocked the door to the store and stepped inside. Through some trick of her imagination, the smoke smelled stronger here than outside.

As Mary Jo rounded the counter she glanced into the case and smiled at the way the security lights sparkled off the jewelry. Brilliant sparks of garnet red and softer ruby, shots of sapphire, the white glare of a diamond, glints of gold and silver. Without pausing she took the hall to the cubbyhole.

There was the backpack, right on the file cabinet where Andy had left it. She picked it up, then paused beside her desk. The inventory paperwork glared at her accusingly. If she'd been able to keep her mind on her work, instead of on a man named Jack, she would have finished the report today. Conscience stinging her, she stuffed the printout and diskette into her coat pocket. She would work on the report on her home computer and have it finished when Bob returned Monday.

At the door to the hall she stopped, her purse hanging from one shoulder, backpack from the other. The smell of smoke was suddenly too strong. Alarmed, she noticed smoke creeping out from beneath the closed door to Bob's office, wafting up to hang along the hall ceiling.

Mary Jo pictured that old space heater Bob kept beneath his desk and groaned. Had he used it today and left it on? She couldn't remember.

She reached for the doorknob . . . The door had been open when she'd locked up. Bob never closed it, and Mary Jo had been the last one out. She knew she hadn't closed it.

Puzzled, but not really expecting more than a smoking space heater, she opened the door. A low sounding *whoosh*, and flames exploded across the room. Their heat and fierceness knocked Mary Jo backward as though she'd been punched in the chest. She stumbled frantically, instinctively away from the fire. It followed her like an enraged beast on the scent of prey.

Back, back, Mary Jo stumbled, until she was back in the cubbyhole at the end of the hall.

*Trapped!*

Afraid to take her eyes off the approaching flames for fear they would leap and attack, Mary Jo reached behind and fumbled for the phone. The line was dead.

*And so am I.*

# TWO

The Two Oaks Fire Chief stood before his cupboard staring at the cans of soup there, trying to decide which one to open for supper, when the alarm came in.

*Jewelry store. Smoke and flames visible.*

In less than two minutes Jack Riley and his team of volunteers were dressed in full turnout gear and screaming out of the fire station in Pumper Number One, with Pumper Number Two and Fire Rescue right behind them. There was no need for directions. There was only one jewelry store in town.

Within another minute and a half Number One screeched to a halt before Two Oaks Gems on the town square. In seconds the fire engine was joined by its fellow fire department vehicles, two police cars, an EMT truck, and, Jack noted as he spotted Faith McShane's car pulling in nearby, the local press.

It looked like they'd all be eating smoke for supper this night.

From the sidewalk in front of the store, the fire appeared to be mainly confined to the back office. Jack shouted orders at his crew—volunteers to the man—to lay hose for a frontal assault. The back alley was too narrow to cuss a cat in, much less park a pumper. He'd send men back there, but he wouldn't mount a two-front attack unless he had to. There was too much likelihood of one group driving the flames and smoke directly at the other.

Men scrambled to obey his commands.

Someone yelled at him. Impatient to be inside battling the blaze, Jack whipped his head around. "What?"

It was Faith McShane. "I think Mary Jo's in there," she cried.

Jack stiffened. Mary Jo? *His* Mary Jo, of the frightened gray eyes and the mouth that had haunted his sleeping and waking hours since the day before?

He couldn't take time to ask questions. All that mattered was that there might be a victim inside. If so, she wasn't in the outer showroom, so she must be good and trapped behind the blaze.

"Let's knock a hole in this beast," he shouted

to the men on the hose. "We have a possible victim."

Jack donned an SCBA—self-contained breathing apparatus—and tank. He issued orders for men on the secondary hoses to wet down the roofs of the connecting buildings and the wooden fence across the alley, as well as the trees there. A fire on the square was a bitch. The buildings were connected for a block at a time, they were old, brittle, and dry. Thank God the exteriors, at least, were brick rather than the one-hundred-year-old wood that made up much of the interiors.

The instant the lines were charged with water the men went in on cue, into the smoke, into the mouth of hell, with Jack at the nozzle leading the way.

Mary Jo tried squatting low against the floor where there might be more air, but the fire seemed somehow closer that way and she felt more vulnerable. So she stood, and coughed, and huddled in the corner, and prayed.

Nothing seemed real to her. Not the flames that trapped her in the corner with their heat and threat, not the sizzle and pop as they devoured carpet and walls, creeping closer and closer to her desk; not the smoke that stung her eyes and choked her. Only her son's backpack, which she clutched to her chest, seemed real.

She was going to die. She didn't see any way around it. The only way out was through the flames, and by now they probably engulfed the entire length of the hall and, for all she knew, the showroom as well. She would never make it.

She couldn't die! She could not leave her babies to become orphans. They'd already lost their father. They couldn't afford to lose her too.

*Think!*

There had to be a way to save herself. But no revelations presented themselves to her. Through the fire was the only way out. She couldn't even see the doorway now for the flames and smoke, and the door was less than ten feet away.

She didn't know which was going to kill her first, the flames, the smoke, or sheer terror.

*Oh, God, not like this. Please don't let me burn alive. Please don't leave my children with that horror.*

Mary Jo closed her eyes against the sting of smoke and tears. Mentally she traced her way around the desk, through the flames at the door, down the hall and into the showroom, around the counter, across the floor, and out the front door past the ugly ficus to precious freedom.

Solid flames, all of it. At least from what she could tell. She would never make it. Already her skin felt as if it would melt from her bones in the heat. And the fire was getting closer. Closer.

She was going to die here in this inferno. She

did not have the nerve to deliberately run into the flames and try to find her way out. It would be suicide. Yet if she stayed where she was, the fire would reach her in seconds. It seemed to be staring at her, stalking her, mocking her puny attempts to breathe searingly hot air, what little air there was. It danced and cackled and waved fiery arms, taunting her, teasing, as though it knew it had her trapped, toying with her like a cat with a mouse. A very large cat; a very small, terrified mouse.

*Dear God!*

She thought she heard shouting, but the roar of the fire and the blood pounding in her ears made it impossible to tell. Was someone out there trying to help her?

"Here! Help! I'm—" Her words ended in a choking gag as smoke once again clogged her throat and lungs.

Then the fire seemed to surge away from her toward the hallway for a moment. It roared. It snapped. And incredibly, Mary Jo felt . . . water?

Suddenly a hole appeared in the flames. Like a knight to the rescue, or the answer to a prayer, the dark shape of a man appeared in the doorway, framed by leaping flames. Moses in a face mask, parting a sea of fire.

For a fleeting second Mary Jo wondered if her mind had snapped, or if the blazing beast had taken human form and was coming after her. But no, this was a man—a fireman in boots, helmet, face mask, rubber coat. Rescue!

Drops of water and streaks of soot partially obscured the face behind the mask, but not even the smoke and flames of the fire could compete with the startling blue eyes that focused sharply on her. He appeared out of the flames and smoke like an apparition, but when he reached for her, his touch was solid and real. And familiar. She swayed into it. An unexpected and totally inappropriate shiver of awareness shimmied down Mary Jo's spine as she recognized those blue eyes.

*Jack.*

In a gesture as natural as breathing, Jack slid his arms around her and held her close. There was fear in those familiar gray eyes the color of smoke, but her mouth and jaw were set with grim determination, as if she would fight the fire herself with nothing more than spit and fists. There was soot on her face, but not a hair was out of place, and her suit had yet to wilt, despite the raging heat. She should have been a wreck, physically and emotionally. That she was neither filled him with admiration and more. What power did this woman named Mary Jo have over him?

*Jeez, Riley,* he thought, *you've probably had more inappropriate thoughts, but not in this lifetime. Keep your mind above your belt and on business before that fire gets the better of both of you.*

For a fleeting instant, he wondered which fire he'd meant. The one at his back that was doing its best to destroy Bob Yates's livelihood, or the fire that surged shockingly in his blood when his eyes connected with those of a woman he'd known approximately twenty-four hours.

When she coughed on a lungful of smoke Jack peeled off his mask and leaned close to place it over her face.

Mary Jo gratefully sucked in clean air. Never had she tasted anything so precious. Never had she seen anything so spellbinding as the incredibly blue eyes of her rescuer. They were both cool and hot, calming and exciting. What a time for her libido to resurrect itself from the cold storage in which it had been for so long.

It was a fluke, that was all. The human body's survival-of-the-species response to being threatened with death. She knew that, yet still she could not take her eyes from his. The effect they had on her now was even more powerful than the day before when he'd kept her calm after the accident.

Flames surged closer, then a hard spray of water shot through. Jack shielded her body with his, protecting her, giving her his own air to breathe.

From somewhere behind him came a hissing, sizzling sound, like the warning burr a rattlesnake gives just before it strikes. With a sharp curse, Jack used his body to push Mary Jo flush against the wall at her back. Tucking her head securely beneath his chin, he used his arms to cover his head.

Mary Jo couldn't breathe. "What—"

"Close your eyes," he shouted, pressing harder against her. In the next instant an explosion slammed through the room. Jack knew the sound. There must have been a breaker box on the wall behind him. It had just blown. The steel cover slammed into the wall mere inches from his head with enough force to have decapitated him. The shock wave shoved him hard against Mary Jo. What little breath she had left her in a harsh *oomph*.

Over the flames at his back, water bounced off the ceiling from where the guys on the hose aimed it to avoid knocking Jack or anyone else off his feet. It showered down on fire, rescuer, and victim alike.

Then, as suddenly as it had flared to life and trapped her in the office, the fire was gone. Smoke still billowed and plumed, but now men were everywhere, shouting, cursing, kicking at smoldering debris along the floor.

"Chief!"

"Yo," Jack answered.

"You okay?"

"We're fine," he called. "Come on," he said to Mary Jo. "Let's get you out of here."

He steadied her with an arm around her shoulders and led her through what was left of the store. Mary Jo told herself she didn't need the support, but she knew she lied. With every step, her knees threatened to buckle as she remembered how close she'd come to dying.

Beyond the front door, the icy January air was more welcome than anything she could imagine. Mary Jo sucked in a deep, cleansing breath, and choked on it.

Jack pounded lightly between her shoulder blades until she caught her breath.

A flash of light went off in her face. Mary Jo blinked and turned her face toward Jack.

At the same time, he moved to shield her. "Knock it off, Faith."

"Sorry." Faith McShane lowered her camera. "But you two just made the front page of the next edition."

"Well, if it's a photo you want," Jack said, not even then realizing what he was about to do, "try this." He turned Mary Jo in his arms, tilted her face toward his with a hand to her soot-covered chin, and kissed her.

Mary Jo was stunned into immobility. She barely knew the man. She didn't like public displays, and the kiss was meaningless, but it didn't feel meaningless. It felt heartstoppingly real and . . . important. It felt hot, elemental. Sexual.

It terrified her.

Before she could gather herself to shove him away, he raised his head and grinned that irre-

sistible grin from the day before. "Yep." He
winked at her.

*Winked.* She couldn't remember the last time
a man had winked at her, and he'd done it twice
in two days.

"I'm ready for that affair whenever you are,
darlin'."


The EMTs checked Mary Jo over, made her
take a few deep breaths of oxygen, then drove
her home, with one of the crew following with
her mother's car. Mary Jo was too shaken to protest any of it.

The problem was, she wasn't sure which had
shaken her more—the fire, the kiss, or finding
out that Jack was the fire chief. She was alive—
for which she was eternally grateful—but that
tiny spark of a dream that had come to life inside
her had been burned to ashes.


"Long night, huh?" Two Oaks Police Chief
Dalton McShane handed Jack a cup of coffee and
offered him a chair before his desk.

"You might say that." The sun was just coming up. Jack sat, took a sip of coffee. The jolt of
hot caffeine was just what he needed to keep him
going long enough to get home and avoid
drowning in his own shower before he tackled
the rest of the day.

"I assume you've been at the fire scene all night. What did you find?"

"Too much."

Dalton sat behind his desk. "Arson?"

"Arson."

"You're sure?"

"Positive." Jack laid the details out for him. Dalton cursed.

"My sentiments exactly. What do you know about the woman who was trapped in there?"

Dalton's lips quirked. "Mary Jo? Don't look at me. You're the one who kissed her."

Jack grinned. "I couldn't help myself. Call it the heat of the moment."

Dalton groaned. Firefighters came up with the worst puns.

"I only did it to give your wife a good picture for the paper."

"I'm sure my wife thanks you, even if Mary Jo doesn't."

"Mary Jo . . . ?"

"Simpson. She's Arliss Kelley's daughter."

"I don't think I wanted to hear that." Frowning, Jack took another sip of coffee. He knew Arliss Kelley through his parents. She was one of his mother's best friends. He remembered Jeff Kelley, a couple of years behind him in school, but he couldn't remember ever knowing Jeff's little sister, Mary Jo.

"You're not suggesting Mary Jo started that fire, are you?"

Jack shrugged. "Ninety percent of the time, the person who discovers the fire and reports it turns out to be the one who set it."

"The way I heard it, she discovered it, all right, by being trapped by it. She isn't the one who reported it."

"Still, I'd like to talk to her. You probably ought to be there when I do."



Mary Jo rolled over with a groan, not yet ready to face the day. But the sun bouncing off her dresser mirror straight into her eyes would not be ignored.

Why was her head throbbing like she'd been on a two-day drunk? Why did her throat feel like she'd swallowed ground glass?

Rolling over again, she caught a whiff of smoke. Memory came at once and she sat bolt upright, then grabbed at her head to still the pounding.

Smoke. Fire. The store.

Jack. *That kiss.*

She wouldn't think about it, nor about the disappointing fact that he was a firefighter. Was, in fact, the fire chief. She wouldn't think about him at all.

She wondered if she'd remembered to thank the EMTs who'd brought her and her mother's car home last night. She'd been such a wreck that she'd scared the babysitter and the kids half to death when she'd stumbled into the house reeking of smoke and covered with soot.

Mary Jo's mother had heard about the fire before Mary Jo even made it home. She'd had a neighbor bring her over and arrived just after the EMT truck left.

What little strength Mary Jo had left after getting home last night she'd used to calm everyone and assure them that she was all right. Her mother, bless her, hadn't bought the act for a minute and had stayed for the night. Mary Jo could hear her now downstairs in the kitchen banging away. Arliss Kelley was not a quiet cook. And from the sound of things, she was getting help from the kids.

Mary Jo knew she needed to get downstairs. Andy was only nine and Heather six, so they might not have a clue as to what had nearly happened to her last night, especially since she'd glossed over it. But they understood enough to be afraid. She'd seen the uncertainty in their eyes.

For months after Al's death neither child had wanted Mary Jo out of sight for a minute, afraid that she, too, would leave them, as their father had. That look was back in their eyes last night. She needed to spend time with them, and with her mother, let them see that she was alive and well, let her appreciate just being alive and with her family.

But first she had to have another shower. She

could still smell smoke even though she'd stood beneath the spray last night until all the hot water was gone.

By the time she had nearly drained the hot water tank again with three thorough soapings of her hair and body, Mary Jo felt almost human. She stepped into the kitchen with no makeup, wearing old jeans and a faded sweatshirt, with her hair still wet and slicked back.

Three pairs of eyes turned toward her, each holding its own version of anxiety.

Arliss was the first to speak. "You look pale, honey."

"I'm fine, Mother."

"Are you sure? You could have slept longer."

"I'm fine," Mary Jo repeated firmly, sending her mother a message with her eyes. *Stop it. You're scaring the children.*

"Do you feel bad, Mommy?" Heather's big eyes nearly took up her whole face.

"No." Mary Jo bent down and kissed her daughter on the cheek, then rumpled Andy's hair. He made a face and squirmed out of reach, but she knew he'd already decided that kisses were for babies. He was probably still embarrassed at letting her kiss him last night in front of his grandmother. "I feel absolutely fine. I promise." It wasn't too much of a lie.

"Grandma made pancakes." Andy proved it by shoveling a forkful of syrupy pancake into his mouth.

"I helped," Heather proclaimed.

Mary Jo smoothed Heather's hair and shot her mother a look of amusement. "I'm sure you were a big help, sweetie."

Andy snorted in disgust. Then his face lit. "Did you remember to get down on the floor in the fire like I told you so you could breathe?"

"I remembered." It wasn't a lie. She had remembered. She just hadn't been able to do it for long.

"Cool. Wait'll I tell the guys at school. All that stuff Chief Jack told us really works, huh?"

Mary Jo remembered then. Right after school had started last fall Andy had come home one day talking about a demonstration and lecture given to his class by the local fire department. Get down on the floor where there's more air, less smoke. Andy had spent days crawling through the house on his belly.

And more days, she remembered now with quiet terror, claiming he wanted to be a fireman when he grew up. God forbid. A fireman's chances for getting injured or killed on the job were many times greater than those of a cop.

Please God, let Andy grow up to be a shoe salesman.

*Chief Jack.*

It never occurred to her that the smiling man named Jack she'd met after wrecking her car might be Andy's Chief Jack. Why should it?

She was given a reprieve from more questions when the kids went to sprawl on the floor of the den to watch cartoons. Mary Jo and Arliss were nearly finished cleaning up the kitchen— not only was Arliss a noisy cook, she was a bliss- fully messy one also—when the doorbell rang.

"I'll get it," Andy bellowed, his stocking feet pounding toward the front door.

"Andrew Albert Simpson," Mary Jo called, drying her hands on a dish towel, "don't you dare—"

She was too late, as Andy flung the door wide.

"—open that door," she finished with a growl.

"Now, honey," her mother started.

"Don't now honey me. He knows he's not supposed to open the door unless we know who it is."

"Mary Jo." Arliss shook her head in mock sadness. "This is Two Oaks, not Oklahoma City. What's the worst thing that can happen if Andy opens the front door?"

"Hey, squirt," came a deep voice from the front hall.

"Chief Jack! Hey, Mom, it's Chief Jack!"

"That," Mary Jo told her mother darkly. She did not want to see the man again. Every time she remembered the way she'd grinned at him after the car accident, the way they'd joked about having an affair, *the way he'd kissed her*, she felt like a fool.

*A damn firefighter.*

"Jack?" Arliss smiled and tossed down her towel as she headed toward the front of the house. "Jack Riley, is that you?"

"Is that Chief McShane?" Andy's voice rose with excitement. "It is! Mom, the fire chief *and* the police chief. Cool!"

Mentally trying to realign Jack's place in her mind to one of "acquaintance" rather than a man who made her pulse flutter, Mary Jo resignedly put down her dish towel. She supposed Jack and Dalton were here to ask her about the fire. She might as well get it over with. At the least, she owed Jack her thanks.

"Mom," Andy cried when she stepped into the hall. "It's Chief Jack, Mom, and Chief McShane."

"Yes." Mary Jo's gaze barely skimmed Jack and settled on Dalton. "I can see that."

"Did you come about the fire?" Andy was so excited he was practically dancing. "Was it a big one? Was there sirens and ladders and everything?"

"*Were* there sirens," Mary Jo corrected automatically.

"I asked first," Andy protested. "Besides, you were there," he told his mother. "You got to see it in person an' everything. I didn't even get to see it on TV or nothin'."

"I would just as soon have missed the opportunity," Mary Jo muttered.

Heather, looking more anxious than excited, tugged on Andy's arm and whispered something in his ear, all the time casting careful glances at Jack.

Suddenly Andy sobered. Looking up at Jack, he asked, "Are you the one who saved our mother last night?"

Jack's lips twitched. "I seem to be making a habit of it."

With a small gulp, Andy rubbed his palm down the thigh of his jeans then held his hand out to Jack. "Thank you, sir."

Jack frowned, but shook Andy's hand. "You're quite welcome, but you're supposed to call me Jack, remember?"

Blushing and grinning fiercely, with eyes overbright, Andy nodded. "Yes, sir. I mean Jack."

Heather crooked her finger at Jack and asked him to lean down. Smiling, Jack complied. Heather placed a solemn kiss on Jack's cheek. "Thank you for saving our mommy. Are you a hero?"

This time it was Jack who blushed. "Just a firefighter."

"Same thing," Andy proclaimed.

"We're sorry to bother you," Dalton said to Mary Jo, "but we need to ask you a few questions."

"Certainly." Without meeting Jack's gaze

Mary Jo motioned the two men toward the living room.

"Neat." Andy made as if to follow, with Heather at his heels.

"Oh no you don't." Mary Jo took each one gently by the arm and turned them back toward the den. "Your job this morning is to watch cartoons."

"Jeez, Louise, Mom, you never let me have any fun."

"I know. I'm a real slave driver."

Heather blinked. "Are we your slaves, Mommy?"

Mary Jo sighed. Heather took everything so literally. "It was just a joke, sweetie, a figure of speech."

Jack watched her herd the kids down the hall. Cute kids, he thought, remembering the small hand held out to shake his, the tiny finger luring him close, the sweet childish kiss on his cheek. Two pairs of young, gray eyes, just like their mother's. But unlike their mother's eyes, the kids' eyes had been filled with awe. Kids sometimes felt that way around firefighters. Jack didn't think he'd ever get used to the way it made his chest swell with pride and emotion.

But their mother hadn't looked at him with awe. She hadn't looked at him at all. That worried him.

"Here," Arliss said to him and Dalton. "Let me take your coats."

She hung their coats on pegs in the hall, then led them into the living room.

"Make yourselves at home and I'll get us all a cup of coffee."

"Thanks," Dalton told her. "We'd appreciate it."

Jack took the opportunity while waiting to look around. He admitted he was curious about Mary Jo Simpson. Jack knew a lot of women, and planned to know a lot more of them in the years to come. But it was rare that a woman he'd spent so little time with could capture and hold his attention to the extent Mary Jo had.

The last time he'd been so obsessed had ended up in nothing less than disaster. The implications of this time were frighteningly similar, yet different. He had an arson to investigate, and the only witness to the fire would not meet his eyes.

Dammit. He didn't want her to be the one. But Jack knew better than to dismiss obvious signs. He'd learned that rule the hard way. He would just have to do his job, forget about how attractive the prime suspect was.

Jack scanned the room.

Nice room, soft, floral furnishings with glass and brass accents. A fireplace.

On the mantel were three United States flags. Each was folded into a regulation triangle and encased in Lucite, and each bore a discrete brass plaque at its base. Tucked in behind a corner of each plaque was a wallet-sized snapshot of a man. At a guess, he'd say that the flags had once been draped over coffins. He started to step closer to read the plaques and study the photos when Arliss returned with the coffee.

"Here we go. Oh, and there you are, honey," she added when Mary Jo entered.

Arliss filled cups and passed one to each of them before taking one for herself. She motioned Jack and Dalton to have a seat on the sofa, while she sat in the wingback chair beside the fireplace. She started to take a sip, then stopped and rested the cup on her knee. When she raised her head she sought Jack with damp eyes. "You will never know," Arliss said quietly, a hitch in her voice, "how grateful I am, Jack."

Mary Jo was surprised to see that masculine face with its calm eyes and cocky mouth turn red with a blush for the second time that morning. Jack gave a simple nod. Then his gaze found Mary Jo and those calm eyes turned hot and teasing. "It was my pleasure."

His smooth, deep voice sent shivers of heat down her spine and memories of his kiss tingling across her lips. She resented it. She didn't want to be—refused to be—attracted to a man with a job like his. No one in his right mind deliberately rushed into a fire. Such an act was contrary to every survival instinct of any living creature, except maybe a moth. Firefighters were as crazy as cops. Crazier. Mary Jo wanted nothing to do with either ever again.

She turned away and paced toward the front window. "You said you had questions?"

Jack noted the tension in her voice, her shoulders. "Yes. I have questions." He set his cup on the coffee table and pulled a small notebook from his shirt pocket. "Can you tell us how the fire started?"

Mary Jo took the recliner across from the sofa. "I assume it was that old space heater Bob kept under his desk."

"It was faulty?"

Mary Jo shrugged. "It was old. Every now and then Bob had to kick it to get it to come on or go off."

Jack ground his teeth and made a note on his pad. He couldn't count the number of times sheer foolishness, such as continued use of a faulty electrical appliance, ended up being the direct cause of disaster. It could have been this time, but it wasn't. He already knew the heater wasn't what started the fire. "Your car, or rather, your mother's car," he said, "was in front of the store with the engine running."

"Yes. Andy came by after school and left his backpack. When I stopped for groceries on the way home I remembered that I'd left it."

"So you went back."

"Yes."

"You entered by the front door?"

"That's the only key I have. I'm not sure there is a key to the back door. We never use it."

Somebody *had* used that door, according to Dalton, but Jack would let him decide whether to mention it if he wanted to. "So you entered by the front door, then ended up trapped in the back office by the fire. How did that happen?"

The memory of the fire leaping toward her sent chills down Mary Jo's arms, but she managed to explain how she'd come to be trapped. "I didn't realize there was a fire until I—oh, I nearly forgot!" She stiffened. "Bob's office door was closed."

"You said that," Jack told her. "You opened the door and the fire exploded, you said."

"A flash?" Dalton asked Jack.

"It could have happened."

Mary Jo blinked. He didn't believe her! The sorry s.o.b. thought she was lying!

"The fire could have smoldered in the closed room," Jack offered Dalton. "Ate up all the oxygen, then smoldered some more, just waiting for the influx of fresh air. Then, flash. Usually takes a little longer than a few minutes to build up, though."

Mary Jo shook her head. "But the door shouldn't have been closed. Bob never shuts it, and I was the last one to leave and I know it was open then. But when I came back it was closed." Finally the true reason for Jack and Dalton's visit became clear. "It wasn't an accident, was it?

Someone set that fire. But why? It makes no sense. If someone went to the trouble to break into the store, why bother with a fire? There is thousands of dollars worth of jewelry in the display case."

"Mary Jo," Dalton began, setting his cup down. "The safe was open."

"The safe is always open these days. It's broken."

Jack's eyebrows hiked. "A jewelry store with a broken safe?"

"Was it empty?" Mary Jo asked cautiously, afraid she already knew the answer.

"Nothing in it but smoke. Do you know what was there?"

Mary Jo swallowed hard. "We got a new shipment of Rolex watches just before closing. I put them in the safe myself. Have you contacted Bob?"

"We located him this morning," Dalton told her. "He'll be back tonight."

"Then I guess I don't have much time. I better get down there right away."

"To the store?" Jack asked. "Why?"

"To clean up as much as possible—"

Dalton was shaking his head before she finished. "I can't let you do that, Mary Jo. Not until we've finished investigating."

"Oh." Mary Jo swallowed. The store was a crime scene. She should have thought of that. "Robbery."

"And arson." Jack narrowed his eyes at her.

"Are you sure it was arson?" Mary Jo asked, not wanting to believe it. "The heater . . ."

"Was old and should have been replaced," Jack said tersely. "And it was the first thing to go up, but it didn't go up on its own."

"What do you mean?" Mary Jo demanded.

"There might have been a little spontaneous combustion going on in front of the camera after the fire, but the only spontaneous combustion at work inside that building was when the match hit the gasoline."

Mary Jo nearly spilled her coffee. "Gasoline?"

"You don't mean it," Arliss protested.

"I do mean it." Jack's voice was hard.

"How can you be sure?" Mary Jo asked. The thought of someone deliberately setting the fire was more than she could absorb.

"Because it soaked through the carpet. The floor underneath is wood. The accelerant found its way down into the cracks between the boards, where air couldn't get to it, where it couldn't burn. It was easy enough to smell once the smoke cleared. What I couldn't figure was why someone would pour gasoline over a metal space heater rather than the wooden desk, or just the carpet."

Mary Jo didn't like the way he was looking at her, as though he found his answers on her face.

"It makes sense," Jack went on without

prompting, "only if the arsonist knew the heater was bad and thought as long as it went up first, no one would bother investigating further."

"Now wait just a minute." Mary Jo jumped from her chair, chest heaving. "I don't think I like what you're insinuating."

"I wouldn't presume to insinuate." Jack leaned back on the sofa and watched her through narrowed eyes.

"Oh, yes, you would. You seem to make a habit of presuming."

He raised an eyebrow in question.

"You presumed I wouldn't mind you kissing me last night in front of half the town," she shot back. An instant later she fiercely wished she could call back her hasty words.

"Yeah." Jack grinned. "And judging by the way you kissed me back, I was right."

Mary Jo started to deny it, but she knew the blush stinging her cheeks gave her away. It was hard to deny the truth. She decided on another direction.

"The only people who knew that heater was bad are Bob and me. The only people who knew the safe didn't lock are Bob, the company in Amarillo that was supposed to fix it last week, and me. Since Bob's in Dallas and the safe man is in Amarillo, I seem to be the only one left, according to your reasoning."

Dalton looked up from his own notepad. "No one's accusing you—"

"He is." Mary Jo pointed a finger at Jack. "Look at him. You can see the wheels turning in that pea-sized brain of his. Well I hate to disappoint you, Chief Riley, but you've got the wrong person. If you'll recall, I was the one trapped in that fire. If I'd set it myself and robbed the safe, I'd damn sure have gotten myself out of there without getting trapped."

"It would have been the smart thing to do."

"Jack," Arliss cried. "You can't possibly believe my daughter . . . well, you just can't, that's all."

"Like Dalton said, Miz Kelley, no one's accusing anyone here of anything. We're just asking questions."

"You've asked your questions," Mary Jo said coldly. "Now get out."

Jack tucked his notebook away and rose slowly from the sofa, never taking his eyes off Mary Jo. "Okay," he said. "We'll go. For now. But we'll be in touch."

In the hallway Mary Jo glared at him. "I didn't start that fire."

"Which fire would that be?" Jack murmured for her ears alone.

Mary Jo ignored the hot shiver that slid up her spine. "I don't know what you're talking about." Her eyes looked everywhere but at him as he put on his coat.

"The one in the jewelry store, or that other one we ignited for the camera?"

Mary Jo stared him straight in the eye. "Like I said, I don't know what you're talking about."

Jack met her gaze. "Oh, I think you do."


"What was that all about?" Dalton asked Jack once they were inside Dalton's black-and-white.

*I wish I knew,* Jack thought. "Nothing."

Nothing is what he should have said to her. His gut told him she was telling the truth, that she knew nothing about the fire, had nothing to do with starting it.

If so, why the tension? Why throw up that brick wall? The woman he'd talked with today was not the same one he'd teased and flirted with two days ago at the corner of Main and Third. That woman had flirted back. She wasn't even the same woman he'd kissed last night for the camera. That woman had kissed him back.

This woman, today, was cold and standoffish. Tense. Angry. Two days ago she'd eaten him alive with her eyes. Last night she'd looked at him as if he were the answer to her prayers. Today she'd looked everywhere but at him until he'd started asking direct questions.

Why? That's what he wanted to know.

Jack was a man who normally trusted his gut, and his gut said she was not the person who set the fire.

But was that his gut speaking, his instincts? Or was that opinion coming from farther south?

He was attracted to her. Maybe this time his gut was lying.

"Is there something personal here I should know about?" Dalton asked.

Jack's "No" came quickly.

"Good. Then maybe you wouldn't mind keeping an eye on her."

"Do what?"

"Jack, ol' buddy, we have an arson and a robbery on our hands. She had opportunity, inside knowledge of what was in the safe and that the safe was broken, and she's a widow with two kids to raise, which means she might even have a motive for stealing a shipment of very expensive watches."

Jack's throat closed. He'd thought of every one of those points himself, and they made him sick to his stomach. But his stomach and his libido had no place in this. Someone had set a fire in his town. This was his job. "I'll see what I can do."

# THREE

*. . . or that other one we ignited for the camera?*

No matter how many times Mary Jo shoved Jack's taunting comment to the back of her mind, it kept springing free to haunt her, tease her.

Okay, so she'd been attracted to him. So his eyes had calmed and heated her, his smile had curled her toes. So his kiss had made her mind go numb.

So what?

He was a firefighter. And he thought she was an arsonist. Maybe even a thief. End of story. She had let her imagination run wild for a day or two. No big deal. It was over now. She was sane again.

And how dare he practically accuse her of setting the store on fire one minute, then tease her about that kiss the next?

She was not the least surprised by the
amount of bold, angry red that showed up in her
painting Saturday night after the kids were in
bed. She was angry. With the world, fate, herself. Jack. Al, for getting himself killed and leaving her lonely so she could be tempted by an
engaging grin.

Damn right she was angry.

None of which explained what that small
splash of yellow was doing in the center of the
red.

Sunday morning Mary Jo forgot all about
that troubling spot of yellow. A south wind had
swept in during the night, and with it came
warm air from the Gulf of Mexico. The steady
plop of water dripping off the roof as ice melted
was welcome music. The only yellow she noticed
was the buttery yellow of the warm winter sun.

Even the children warmed her that morning
by being ready for church by the time Arliss
came to pick the three of them up. Andy even
announced that he'd already checked to make
sure the back door was locked without being
told.

Sunday morning saw some of the heaviest
traffic each week in Two Oaks as most families
made their way to the church of their choice.
Mary Jo's neighborhood practically emptied itself, even more so today than usual, probably be-

cause of the sudden welcome change in the weather.

George Schaeffer, the minister at the First Baptist Church, extended his hands toward Mary Jo and offered her a concerned smile. "Praise the Lord that you're all right."

"Thank you," Mary Jo murmured.

"Gave us all a fright, that's for sure," Verna Sneed added from where she stood beside the minister at the door of the church.

"I'll say." Venita, Verna's sister, gave a sharp nod of her head, hard enough to send a silver-blue curl tumbling onto her forehead.

"Lands, yes." Viola, the third sister, pulled Mary Jo's hand out of the preacher's grasp. "When we heard you were trapped in that fire, why, we were absolutely horrified."

"So was I." Mary Jo gave them a rueful smile. "But I'm fine, really."

Viola arched a brow as a smile teased her lips. "You certainly are, thanks to a certain young, good looking, *single* fire chief." Viola patted her chest and rolled her eyes. "What a hunk."

"Oh, my, yes." Venita's smile bordered on the benign. "He is quiet a specimen, our Jack."

"Sisters." Verna puckered her lips. "You forget yourselves. Well hello, Chief Riley. My, that was fine work you and your young volunteers did Friday night, saving our Mary Jo and the jewelry store."

Mary Jo cringed as Jack joined them on the steps.

"Why, thank you, ladies." Jack grinned that grin, the one that once had weakened Mary Jo's knees by turning them to water but now made her feel like smacking him a good one. To her great discomfort, Jack followed her and her family into the church. To her further dismay, he sat in their pew. The nerve of the man!

Yet she didn't dare say anything with all these people around, and Jack probably knew that, the creep. She found it difficult to keep Christian-like thoughts in her head when the man who thought she was a criminal was sitting so close. There was no one between her and him except Andy. And Andy, who had no idea what Jack thought of his mother, was looking at Jack like he was Superman, Spiderman, and the Lone Ranger all rolled into one.

Mary Jo fought a shiver. She didn't want Andy idolizing a firefighter. That was even worse than his determination to be a cop when he grew up. She'd been praying he would outgrow that, but this was too much.

*Be careful what you wish for* . . .

Next time, she reminded herself, she would be more specific in her prayers.

Blue-haired Venita, Verna, and Viola, The Sisters, as the eighty-two-year-old triplets were called, filed into the pew in front of the one Mary Jo and her family had taken. With them was their older brother, Vincent. Vincent was usually with his sisters as, to hear him tell it, they were entirely too reckless behind the wheel of a car. Viola, he liked to complain, did "forty heart-stopping miles per hour!" one time out on the state highway. These days Vincent drove them everywhere they wanted to go in their twelve-year-old Lincoln at a steady and sedate thirty-five.

After taking their seats, the Sisters, as one, turned and eyed Jack sitting next to Andy. Their smiling, rheumy-eyed gazes slid to Mary Jo, then back to Jack, before Vincent drew their attention by clearing his throat much more loudly than necessary. Verna tittered and was the first of the three to look away and face forward. Viola shot Mary Jo another look, smiled, and turned away.

Venita winked at her. "Looks like you've got a live one. If you're smart, you won't let him get away."

"Sister," Vincent hissed.

The heat that stung Mary Jo's cheeks was that of pure rage. She shot Jack a killing look. Over Andy's head, he grinned back at her.

Mary Jo spent the next hour and a half grinding her teeth. She supposed it wouldn't be very Christian-like to pray for his end of the pew to catch on fire, so she heroically restrained herself from the urge. But maybe a hole in the floor, just big enough for him to disappear through . . .

All the way home from church Andy rattled on about getting to sit next to Chief Jack. Even Heather, usually more reserved than her brother, seemed excited that Jack had sat with them during the service, even though she herself had sat between Mary Jo and Arliss.

Mary Jo bit the inside of her jaw for six blocks to keep from saying what she thought of Chief Jack. Chief Jerk was more like it.

But Heather was also more attuned to the people around her than was Andy. "What's the matter, Mommy, don't you like Fireman Jack?"

"It's Chief Jack," Andy corrected. "And of course Mom likes him. Don't you, Mom?"

Mary Jo forced a smile. Her children did not know what Jack thought of her, and she'd just as soon keep it that way. "I hardly know him, Andy."

"But you like him, don't you?" Andy insisted.

For one wistful second, Mary Jo let herself remember the day of the accident, the way those startlingly blue eyes had both calmed and warmed her, the way her heart had lifted at the possibilities of a man like Jack. The way her blood had sang and her body came to life. The way her pulse had raced every time he'd grinned that grin.

She remembered her first sight of him when he'd stepped through the flames in her office like

Moses parting the Red Sea. The ramifications of his chosen profession had not dawned on her by then. She'd been too glad to be rescued, somehow thrilled that it was Jack doing the rescuing.

And that kiss, out on the sidewalk in front of half the town. That kiss that had curled her toes.

All these thoughts rushed through her in a heartbeat. Then reality returned. The questions, the insinuations. And even without them, there was still the determination that a firefighter was absolutely positively the last man on earth she would ever willingly let into her life.

"Mom?"

"I'm sure he's a very nice man."


As usual after church, Arliss went home with Mary Jo and the kids for Sunday dinner. While the kids went to change clothes, Mary Jo went to the kitchen to put the chicken in the sink to soak. Something nagged at the back of her mind, but it wasn't until the chicken was unwrapped and soaking in cold water and Mary Jo was drying her hands that she realized the back door was slightly ajar.

*Dammit, Andy.* She was going to have to talk to him about his carelessness. She'd lived in the city and been married to a cop too long to be able to tolerate such a lapse, no matter how quiet and trouble free Two Oaks was, as her mother kept reminding her.

Trouble free, she thought as she made her way upstairs to change out of her church clothes. According to Jack and Dalton, they had an arsonist and a thief running around. She wouldn't call that trouble free. They thought she was the culprit. She wouldn't call that trouble free.

By the time she was back downstairs Andy and Heather had changed into play clothes and were already outside. Their shrieks of laughter as they took turns leaping into the pile of leaves in the far corner of the backyard echoed across the neighborhood.

No, she thought, she wouldn't say anything to Andy this time about the back door being open. He was undoubtedly distracted by the car accident and the fire. And having what he considered two genuine heroes—the fire chief and the Chief of Police—come knocking on his very own door was enough to distract any red-blooded boy. She couldn't bring herself to scold him. This time. Not when her heart swelled at the sound of childish laughter from a pile of dead leaves.

From the pantry Mary Jo brought out the ten-pound bag of potatoes, then started removing the chicken piece by piece from the water and placing it on a three-ply thickness of paper towels to drain. At the next shriek from the backyard she shook her head, but only partly at herself for her indulgence of Andy's neglect. That pile of leaves had been covered in the same thick layer of ice as had everything else in town, until the warm wind blew in during the night. The ice was all melted now. The pile was a soggy mess. So, too, were her children after the first leap.

"I guess you're not going to tell me unless I ask."

Having thought her mother was still in the bathroom, Mary Jo dropped a chicken breast back into the sink at sound of her voice. The resultant splash pinged her in the eye. She gasped in surprise.

"That was . . . interesting."

"You scared the life out of me. I thought you were still in the bathroom."

"Sorry. Here. I'll do that." Arliss crossed to the sink and plucked the chicken from Mary Jo's grasp. "You talk. What's going on with you and the town hunk?"

"Mother!"

Arliss smirked. "I notice you didn't have to ask who I meant. I didn't know you knew him."

"Presuming you're talking about Jack Riley, what makes you think I do?"

"Well, if what I heard about the picture that's sure to cover the front page of the next *Register* is true—the two of you lip-locked—I certainly hope you know him."

"Mother!"

"What?"

"Lip-locked?"

Arliss frowned. "Did I get it wrong? You know what I mean. Kissing."

*"Lip-locked?"*

"Don't change the subject, dear. What," she said, peering at Mary Jo over the tops of her glasses, "is going on with you and Jack Riley? Not that I'm against something going on. I've been wanting to introduce the two of you for months."

"Mother, the man thinks I'm a thief and an arsonist!"

Arliss frowned and pulled a chicken thigh from the sink. "That was rather the way things went yesterday, but I just can't believe he seriously thinks such a thing. Jack's much too smart for that."

"You could have fooled me," Mary Jo muttered.

Arliss pulled the plug to drain the sink. "You didn't answer my question."

"What question?" Mary Jo asked irritably.

"Why were you kissing Jack Riley on the town square?"

Mary Jo didn't know what made her say it. The words just came out. "I wasn't kissing him on the town square. I was kissing him on the lips."

Arliss whooped with laughter. "I stand corrected. But you're still evading my question."

"I wasn't kissing him." Mary Jo started sorting through the potatoes, picking out the best size for boiling. "He was kissing me."

"The way I heard it—"

"You hear too much."

"—it was not only mutual, but some sort of reference was made to an impending affair?"

"Yes, I heard that too." Mary Jo picked out enough potatoes to mash for dinner, then returned the bag to the pantry. "I believe I just might have to kill him for it."

Arliss tsked. "I can't imagine him saying such a thing to a woman he'd never met before."

"I didn't say we'd never met."

When Mary Jo did not elaborate, Arliss gave a heavy sigh.

"It's no big deal." Mary Jo took the potato peeler from the drawer and started peeling the potatoes. With a sigh of her own, she gave in and told her mother about meeting Jack.

"*He's* the man who helped you at the accident? I might have known."

"Why do you say that?"

"Because aside from being the town hunk, Jack Riley is the nicest, most helpful young man I've ever known."

"He thinks I'm a criminal!"

"Well, we'll just have to straighten that out, won't we? In any case, you were avoiding his gaze yesterday before he ever spoke. *That's* what I'm asking about."

Mary Jo was saved from having to answer her

mother's question by Andy and Heather bounding through the back door shrieking and laughing. With a sigh that was part a daughter's relief, part a mother's dismay, she turned and took in the scene. "Good grief, you just put those clothes on twenty minutes ago, and look at you." To soften her words, she smiled. "Go get cleaned up, both of you."

"Yes, ma'am." Andy grinned and dashed toward his room.

"He stuffed wet leaves down my back." Heather gave an angelic smile. "So I stuffed some down his pants."

Mary Jo and Arliss managed to hold back their laughter until Heather was out of the room. After they were through snickering a moment later, the two women worked together to finish preparing the meal. While mashing the potatoes, Mary Jo heard the kids' voices from the front of the house and knew they had finished changing clothes. It was a couple of minutes before she realized there was a third voice, deep and male, coming from the front hall.

"Who—"

"Hey, Mom," Andy called from the doorway, excitement in his voice. "Chief Jack's here again."

Mary Jo's nerve endings twitched. Every single one of them. She braced herself and turned slowly toward the door. She was definitely going to have to have a talk with Andy and Heather about letting people into the house without her permission. This was just too much! The nerve of the man.

"Jack." Arliss wiped her hands on a dish towel. "Did you come to ask my daughter more of your ridiculous questions?"

Jack gave a good imitation of a sheepish grin. "You're not going to hold it against me because I'm just doing my job, are you?"

"What kinds of questions?" Andy wanted to know.

"No questions," Mary Jo said. She did not want this subject broached in front of her children. If Jack Riley wanted to live to make it out the door he'd just come in, he would read that sentiment in her face and keep his mouth shut around Andy and Heather.

"Your mom's right, squirt. No questions today." Jack arched his neck and peered toward the stove. "Is that your fried chicken, Miz Kelley? That recipe that won the blue ribbon at the county fair last summer?"

"Hey, Mom." Andy was practically dancing with excitement. "Can Jack stay for dinner? Can he, huh?"

Bracing her hands against the counter at her back, Mary Jo faced Jack. "I'm sure he can't stay, Andy."

"Oh, but I can." Jack grinned, his eyes daring Mary Jo to protest. "I really just came by on a neighborhood inspection, but whatever you're fixing smells too good to pass up. Thanks. I appreciate the invitation. Especially since everybody out at Mom and Dad's has got the flu, so I can't go out there and mooch a meal."

"So you thought you'd come here and get Andy to—"

"Mary Jo," Arliss said, cautioning her with a look.

Mary Jo silently ground her teeth again. Her mother was right. She didn't want to let Andy and Heather know their newest hero thought their mother was an arsonist. It would break their hearts and confuse them to no end. With a sigh of defeat, she turned and set an extra place at the table. "What kind of neighborhood inspection?"

"All *right*." Andy jumped and punched the air with his fist.

Jack grinned at Andy. To Mary Jo he said, "Smoke alarms. I see you've got one in here." He nodded toward the unit mounted above the kitchen door leading into the hallway. "How's the battery?"

Before Mary Jo could answer he reached up and pressed the test button. The shrill beep had everyone cringing and covering their ears. Andy and Heather shrieked with laughter.

Jack gave Mary Jo another one of those "I dare you to say anything" grins. "That one checks out."

Mary Jo gave him a tight smile. "Andy, while

we get dinner on the table why don't you and Heather show Jack the rest of the smoke alarms?"

"Cool. C'mon, Jack."

Jack had barely left the doorway when Arliss pounced. "Say what you want, but not only do I think he doesn't believe you're a criminal, I think he's sweet on you."

"Mother!"

"Yes?" Arliss said, smiling sweetly.

"I will not discuss this with you. There's nothing to discuss. Just fry the damn chicken and shut up."

Arliss's smile widened. "Whatever you say, dear."

Jack willingly followed Andy and Heather from room to room. He didn't mind that he was getting a detailed tour instead of just being shown the smoke alarms. It fit in with his plans to get to know Mary Jo Simpson better. He was curious as to how a widow with two young children could afford a house that was less than five years old, and a car that had looked brand new, on the paltry salary Bob Yates must be paying her.

More questions arose as the kids led him from room to room. The den boasted a large-screen televison, personal computer, and extensive sound system. In Andy's room sat another computer, plus the latest handheld electronic game unit, and three pairs of expensive athletic shoes that he would surely outgrow in a few months. In Heather's room, through her open closet door, Jack saw a row of frilly dresses, and along the walls an extensive collection of dolls.

Mary Jo's room caused him considerable discomfort. First, because he knew she wouldn't appreciate her kids taking a stranger there. Second, it was a little more personal than he'd anticipated. Woman things. Cosmetics. Dusting powder. Perfume. He could smell her here, and her scent reminded him of her taste, and he was trying his damnedest to forget both.

At the sight of a minuscule pair of lace panties laying on the foot of her king-sized bed, his heart kicked his rib cage.

"Here's the last smoke alarm." Andy pointed to the unit just outside her bedroom door.

There was one room remaining at the other end of the hall whose door was closed. "What's in there?" Jack asked.

Andy shrugged. "Mom's stuff."

"We're not allowed to go in there," Heather told him solemnly.

What did she keep in there that even her children couldn't see? It was all Jack could do to keep from opening the door of that room.

"Come on, Jack." Andy tugged on his arm. "We forgot to show you the living room."

"I've seen the living room."

"But I bet you didn't check the smoke alarm."

"I bet you're right."

The kids were so great, Jack thought as he followed them back downstairs. It did something to a man's ego to be looked up to with the respect and awe he saw in Andy and Heather's eyes. He felt like a lowlife for using them to learn about their mother, suspecting their mother of the things he suspected her of.

He guessed suspected was too strong a word, but he couldn't let go of the possiblity that she might have needed the extra money a stolen shipment of Rolex watches could bring. Nice people did worse things every day of the week.

"There it is." Heather, with her shy little voice, pointed to the smoke alarm just inside the door to the living room.

"All right. Last one. Ready?" He put his finger on the test button and waited for Heather and Andy to cover their ears, as they'd done with each test.

"Chief Jack?" Little Heather tugged on the sleeve of his flannel shirt.

Jack couldn't resist the shy plea in her eyes. He squatted down to her level. "What is it, sweetheart?"

"Can I do it?"

"Push the button?"

"Uh-huh."

"I don't see why not." Jack swung her up by the waist so she could reach the button.

The girl shrieked with laughter, and her eyes grew wide. "Wow, I'm really up here, aren't I?"

"Do it, Heather," Andy cried, laughing. "Push it. On three, okay? One . . . two . . . three!"

Heather pushed the button and the test beep shrilled through the house. She squealed and clapped her hands as Jack lowered her to stand beside him.

"That was fun, Chief Jack. Thank you."

"You're welcome," he said, thinking he'd never seen a sweeter child, and feeling more rotten by the minute.

"Did you see our flags, Jack?" Andy pointed to the three flags on the mantel that Jack had noticed the day before.

"I saw them yesterday, but I didn't get to look at them," Jack told him as he crossed to the fireplace.

"Grandma calls this our shrine."

Jack winced at Andy's explanation.

"This one," Andy said, pointing to the flag on the right, "is for Uncle Jeff."

The plaque read Jeff Kelley. Jack had known it would. He remembered Jeff from high school. Jeff had been two years younger than Jack, so they hadn't really hung out together much. Jack remembered his mother telling him about Jeff getting killed in Desert Storm while Jack was working for the Dallas Fire Department.

"We never knew him," Heather said. "Grandma says we missed a treat."

"You sure did."

"Did you know him?" Andy's eyes widened. "Did you know our Uncle Jeff?"

"He was a couple of years behind me in high school." Jack stared at the photo of Jeff Kelley in his snappy marine uniform. "I have to agree with your grandmother. You missed a treat. Jeff Kelley was a nice guy."

Jack looked at the next plaque, but knew before he read it that it had to belong to Tom Kelley, Arliss's late husband.

"That's Grandad." Andy's voice was hushed. "I was pretty little when he died, but I remember him. He was really big and strong."

"Yeah," Jack said, a pain blooming in his chest for all these two, and Mary Jo and Arliss, had lost. Texas State Trooper Tom Kelley had been killed on the job about a year before Jack moved back to Two Oaks. The photo was like Jeff's, a formal pose in uniform. "He was a good man."

"You knew Grandpa too?" Heather asked him. "Did you know our daddy?"

"No, I never met your daddy, sweetheart."

Al Simpson, the plaque read. This photo was an informal snapshot of a smiling, good looking man who obviously felt something special for the person behind the camera. Mary Jo, Jack assumed.

"He was a nice man, too," Heather told him.

"Well, now, I guess he'd have to be, for your mom to marry him, right? I bet he was tall."

Andy tilted his head and looked up at Jack. "How come you think so?"

"Because you're tall for your age. I bet you take after him."

Andy beamed with pride. His chest swelled. "Mom says so."

"What's this?" Jack fingered the twisted gold nugget embedded with three stones that hung from a gold chain draped over the plexiglass case containing Al Simpson's flag.

"That's the necklace Mom made for Dad. It's got mine and Heather and Mom's birthstones in it, see?"

"I see. Your mom made this?"

"Yeah, she used to make all kinds of fancy jewelry. I think her awards and things are in her private room, the room we can't go in."

Interesting, Jack thought. A jewelry designer.

"But she doesn't make jewelry anymore," Andy said gravely.

"That's too bad," Jack said, meaning it. "If this is anything to go by, she must have been really good at it."

"Oh, she was," Heather proclaimed. "But her creative juices, along with all her other juices, dried up and went in the grave with Daddy."

Jack choked on a burst of what was surely inappropriate laughter.

"Heather!" came Mary Jo's shocked cry from the doorway.

Heather plopped her hands on her hips and turned to face her mother. "Well, that's what Granny Simpson said when that man kept sending you those pretty flowers and you made the flower man take them back. She said that was why you wanted us to move to Texas, so you could bury yourself—"

"I believe we've all heard more than enough of what Grandmother Simpson had to say." Mary Jo's lips were so puckered up when she spoke that Jack was afraid they were going to disappear.

Beside her, Arliss's eyebrows nearly reached her hairline. "Flowers, Mary Jo?"

Mary Jo's mouth tightened even more. "Chief Riley, I'm sure we've kept you long enough. I'll be glad to send some food home with you."

Jack couldn't help it. He grinned. "Thanks for the offer, but I have plenty of time."

"What about the rest of the neighborhood?" she asked hopefully. "Don't you need to be on about your inspection?"

"Actually," Jack said with as much sobriety as

he could muster under the circumstances, "you were my last stop."

If looks could kill, the one Mary Jo shot him just then would have flayed him alive. This, he thought, had nothing to do with the fire at the jewelry store. This, he decided, both her attempt to get rid of him, and his determination to stay, had to do with the woman. He just couldn't seem to help it, and right then, didn't want to.

Jack stayed for Sunday dinner.

Mary Jo had never been so angry. The sheer nerve of the man! And her mother wasn't helping things one bit.

"So, are you checking the smoke alarms in the entire neighborhood," Arliss asked, "or is there something of particular interest for you at this house?"

"Miz Kelley, you're gonna get me in trouble," he said with a grin.

"Oh?" Arliss paused. "Business, or personal?"

"Mother," Mary Jo ground out.

"Have some more potatoes, Jack. Mary Jo mashed them herself."

"I'm beginning to feel like I'm being trotted out on a leash," Mary Jo muttered.

Andy thought the idea of his mother on a leash was hilarious. Heather just looked puzzled. "How come, Mommy?"

"Never mind, honey." Mary Jo vowed to keep silent the rest of the meal. "It's just a saying."

"You mean like 'pretty is as pretty does'?"

"I was thinking more on the lines of 'a child may have too much of his mother's blessing.' " Mary Jo tossed her mother a dark look.

" 'Never throw stones at your mother,' " Arliss shot back. " 'you'll be sorry for it when she's dead.' "

" 'Never throw stones at your mother,' " Jack added, " 'throw bricks at your father instead.' One of my own mother's favorite sayings," he added with a wink.

"We don't have a father to throw bricks at," Heather said solemnly. "Our daddy died."

Jack's eyes softened as he looked at Heather. "I know. I was sorry to hear about that."

"It was a long time ago," Heather said matter-of-factly. "When I was little. I'm in school now."

"You're still little," Andy said with disgust.

Heather arched her neck in a perfect imitation of Mary Jo when she was angry. "I guess I'm big enough to stuff leaves down your pants. So there."

Jack coughed into his napkin. "Sounds like I missed something."

"I just let her get me so she would quit crying."

"I was not crying."

"Were too."

"Was not."

"That will be enough," Mary Jo said quietly. Jack grinned. Again. "Spoken like a mother."

"I am a mother."

"You're also a woman," Arliss said tartly, "as I keep reminding you."

Jack coughed into his napkin again.

"Thank you, Mother. Isn't it time for you to go home?"

"Of course not." Arliss gave another benign smile. "Andy and Heather are going to help me do the dishes while you take Jack into the living room and entertain him."

"I'm sure Jack needs to be leaving now."

"Actually," Jack said, "as it turns out, I've got plenty of time."

The next thing Mary Jo knew, she and Jack Riley were alone in the living room with sounds floating in from the kitchen of water running, dishes clattering, children laughing.

She didn't waste time. "What are you doing here, Jack?"

Jack wished he had an answer for her. In truth he wasn't sure what had prodded him to come to her house, except for a feeling that things between them weren't as finished as they should be. His gut kept telling him she had nothing to do with the fire or theft. His brain kept warning that that was because he was attracted to her. And he was. He'd felt it again when he caught sight of her after Andy let him in the house. The possibility that he might be wrong, that she might be guilty, made him sick to his stomach.

*Good question, Mary Jo. What the hell am I doing here?* "I told you. Neighborhood inspection."

"That's bull and we both know it."

"Then suppose you tell me why I'm here."

"To snoop around, look for evidence."

It was close enough to the truth that Jack decided he was better off keeping his mouth shut.

Mary Jo's eyes widened. "You really do think I set that fire and stole the watches."

"I never said that."

"You didn't have to. Why else would you be here?"

Jack shrugged and hooked a thumb on his hip pocket. "Maybe because you never got around to telling me when you wanted to start our affair."

"Out," she managed between clenched teeth. "I want you out of this house. I may be forced to bear your presence in public and around my children. I may feel obliged to answer your questions about the fire. But I'll be damned if I'll put up with you ridiculing me in my own home and taking advantage of the fact that my children think you're some kind of hero. If you want to search my house, go ahead. Otherwise, get out."

# FOUR

The focal point of the Two Oaks town square was the new county courthouse, which stretched across the north end of the square. The original one, built in 1898, had been carried off by a tornado in 1914.

The new one, built of native rock so as to hopefully stay put, was started two years later, the year Jack London died, Woodrow Wilson got himself reelected, Pancho Villa crossed the border and raided New Mexico, Boston beat Brooklyn four to one to win the World Series, and Vernon Sneed sank another two dozen oil wells in his back pasture west of town.

It had taken nearly a year to haul in all that rock from the county quarry and marble from up in Colorado and get the courthouse built. It was finished the year John F. Kennedy was born, Buffalo Bill Cody died, and Mata Hari was executed as a spy. That was the year Mary Pickford starred in *The Little Princess* and old George Comstock, God rest his soul, took his wife all the way to Austin to see it.

No sooner was the courthouse finished that year of 1917 when the need came to erect a monument out front to memorialize the names of the local citizens killed in the Great War. They only had two names: Harold Comstock, George's oldest son, and Elliot Salizar, whom nobody these days could quite remember.

As the town fathers that year of 1917 were pretty familiar with the ways of human nature and politics, they left plenty of room on the monument. And a good thing, too, when World War II rolled around not too many years thereafter. The only thing they hadn't thought of was to number that first war.

Mary Jo stood before the monument Monday morning before going to check on the damage caused by the fire. Two names listed under The Great War. Four more for World War II, one for Korea, three for Viet Nam. For Desert Storm, there was only one name. Jeff Kelley, Mary Jo's brother, was the only person from Two Oaks to perish in that hell-baked desert land of the Middle East.

Mary Jo traced her finger along Jeff's name and whispered a prayer. She still missed him, even after several years. She still hated the Marines for luring him in with their "Few Good

Men" slogan, hated that he'd been such a damn good pilot that he'd been needed first in Desert Shield, then Desert Storm. Hated that he hadn't been good enough to avoid being shot down.

"Dammit, Jeff," she said to the marble monument, "why did you have to go off and get yourself killed?"

When no answer came forth, Mary Jo tucked her hands into the pockets of her light jacket— all that she needed since the weather was still unseasonably warm. She turned away from the monument and followed the sidewalk that led through the square block of grass that was the center of the town, both figuratively and literally.

On each side of the sidewalk, neat flower beds lay buried beneath a thick layer of mulch waiting for spring. Beyond them, on each side, stood the two oaks for which the town was named, their tall branches meeting overhead to shade the sidewalk in the summer.

Mary Jo was dawdling, she knew, but she was none too eager to face returning to the scene of the fire just yet. Winter or not, she always drew strength from standing beneath these two trees. There were hundreds of other trees in town, to be sure. But they'd all been planted by human hands.

These two oaks had been planted by God. They'd stood alone on the wide, flat plains, pointing the direction, offering shade and shelter. When the town was first settled, they'd been the only trees in sight. They must have seen so much during their one hundred plus years. Town picnics, speeches by politicians, street dances. Even a hanging once, according to the old photograph on display in the library.

*You're sure in a mood today, Mary Jo.*

She was in a mood, a somber one. It was time to snap out of it and get down to business. Until the jewelry store was repaired she was out of a job. She was supposed to be on her way there to see if she could help in the cleanup and repairs. Instead, she was dawdling in the park.

She dreaded going to the store. The front door was propped open, no doubt to air the place out, and Bob's car was parked in front. How was she going to face him? She hadn't set the fire or stolen the Rolexes, but she had been left in charge. It had happened, as her father would have said, on her watch. She felt responsible for the loss and destruction.

But standing there beneath the oaks wasn't going to accomplish anything. Squaring her shoulders, Mary Jo turned from her contemplation of the oaks and crossed the street to Two Oaks Gems. Or what was left of it.


Jack was just coming out of the courthouse when Mary Jo crossed the street toward the jewelry store. He paused on the steps and watched as she stopped on the sidewalk. She stood there for a long moment staring at the door. She shifted, squared her shoulders. Took a deep breath.

Jack wondered what was going through her mind just then. Was she having to brace herself to walk back into the building where she almost died? Or was she girding herself to brazen it out and return to the scene of her crime?

The investigation of the premises was complete. Dalton had taken the crime scene tape down a couple of hours ago. Bob Yates had already had Chester Dominguez over to inspect the damage and give him an estimate on repairs. Word had it that the insurance adjuster would be by later today or tomorrow.

Jack wished them luck. The showroom suffered only slight smoke and water damage, but Bob's office was a wreck.

He wondered how Mary Jo would react to seeing it.

"Mary Jo," Bob said fervently, clasping her hands as she stepped into the showroom. "Thank God you're all right."

And thank God Bob was out front, she thought, rather than back in his burned out office. Mary Jo wasn't sure she wanted to see exactly what the fire had done.

And thank God Bob didn't seem to think she

had started the fire and stolen the watches. Surely if he shared Jack's suspicions he wouldn't be giving her such a warm greeting.

She smiled. "I'm fine. Really," she assured him. It wasn't much of a lie. "But I'm so sorry, Bob. This is just awful." The lingering smell of smoke made her want to gag as it brought with it memories of the terror of that night.

County Sheriff Harry Yates, Bob's cousin, was with Bob. Sheriff Yates scratched his head. "It's bad enough, but it could have been a lot worse."

Mary Jo shivered at the reminder of how much worse it had almost been. Except for Jack and his volunteer firefighters, she would be dead.

"Nobody was killed and the building's still standing. Everything else, the insurance can take care of." Sheriff Yates was a practical man.

"Praise God," Bob muttered.

"Still makes me mad enough," the sheriff said, "to make me want to find the culprit, pinch his head off, and tell the Good Lord he died."

"Now, Harry. We're all upset by this." Bob sighed and looked around the room. "So much to be done."

"What can I do to help?" Mary Jo asked.

"You can go home and recuperate from this ordeal," Bob told her. "We can't open for business for another week or so anyway."

"But the mess . . ."

"Will be taken care of. That's why we have

insurance. Repairs will start hopefully in a few days, as soon as the adjuster is satisfied with the estimates. I'll have them start here in the showroom first, that way maybe we can open for business while the offices are being repaired."

"But—"

"Home, Mary Jo. Rest. The insurance will even cover your wages while you're off work. There's nothing for you to do here until we're ready to reopen." He gave a rueful smile. "I guess we can have a fire sale. Too bad we don't have those Rolexes."

"I know," Mary Jo said grimly. "I just can't believe this has happened."

"We'll catch the bastard," the sheriff said firmly. "McShane's a good cop, and my department is offering assistance. Don't you worry about a thing, either one of you. We'll catch the culprit who did this."

"You bet we will."

At the sound of Jack's voice behind her in the doorway, Mary Jo clenched her teeth. Did the man have to show up *everywhere*?

Since she was obviously of no use to Bob, Mary Jo said her good-byes and left as fast as she could. She preferred not to be around if Jack was going to start speculating on who set the fire and stole the watches.

Jack watched her hightail it out of the store and bit back a curse. Had that been guilt he'd heard in her voice when she'd told Bob Yates how sorry she was about the fire?

For that matter, had Bob been laying it on a little thick about how the insurance was going to take care of everything? He'd said he was out of town Friday night, but was he really? He couldn't have been more than ten miles past the city limits by the time the fire was set. Maybe he hadn't even been that far.

Maybe, Jack thought with a frown, Bob Yates and Mary Jo Simpson together . . .

He nearly laughed out loud at that idea.

It was either laugh, or gnash his teeth.


Mary Jo took her time walking home, enjoying the weather while it held, wondering what to do with herself until she could go back to work. In the old days she wouldn't have needed anything to do, she would have been at her jewelry designs every moment she could spare, and then some.

The thought of sitting down at her drafting board to sketch out new ideas sent a rush of panic through her veins. If she opened the door to that corner of her mind that used to be filled with ideas, she was terrified that there would be nothing. No flashes of gold, glimpses of sapphire, garnet, topaz, chunks of silver. Only dark emptiness, as there had been the last time she tried.

No, she thought as she entered her house a few minutes later. She wouldn't look. Wouldn't try. Not today.

She went to the laundry room next to the pantry and started a load of clothes in the washer. The walk home had not lightened her thoughts any, but her mind had moved to more current matters. Namely, Jack Riley. A troubling subject, Jack Riley. A troubling man.

Even knowing that he thought she was a thief and an arsonist, even knowing what he did for a living, she still had not been able to stop her internal response when he'd appeared at the jewelry store earlier.

Her heart had given a leap, as though glad to see him. Her blood had rushed, her breathing had hitched. And feelings that had long lay dormant stirred to life, like the embers of a fire long banked and suddenly feeling the rush of air needed to let it breathe again.

Dammit, why did she keep reacting like that to him? Why did she keep remembering his teasing grin and the taste of his kiss? The man was a firefighter, for Pete's sake. He was her accuser. She didn't *want* to be attracted to him.

Shaking the man from her mind wasn't easy. She concentrated on what her hands were doing—folding laundry. Only then did she realize more than an hour had passed since she'd returned home. The first load of laundry was out of the dryer, the second load in, the third in the washer. And she didn't remember doing any of it.

The man was driving her to distraction. He was a menace, and the sooner out of her life, the better.

*Not very damn likely in a town this size.*

The truth of that irritated her.

*Focus,* she reminded herself. Green sock, green—Where was Heather's other green sock?

Over the noise produced by the washer and dryer Mary Jo thought she heard another sound. She stepped out into the kitchen and closed the laundry room door behind her so she could listen.

Hammering.

Someone was . . . hammering on her house?

Leaving Heather's lone green sock on the kitchen counter, Mary Jo rushed out the front door. "What the devil . . ."

Her voice trailed off in shock. Maybe strangled by anger as she took in Jack Riley's shiny red pickup parked in her driveway. The man himself—the jerk who'd all but accused her of being a criminal—stood on a ladder that leaned against her house, hammering a nail in to hold her loose gutter in place.

Mary Jo had been meaning to fix that gutter herself since last fall when she'd discovered it was loose. That Jack Riley would take it upon himself to do it infuriated her.

"What the hell do you think you're doing?" she demanded.

Jack pulled the nail from between his teeth. About damn time. He'd wondered how long he would have to hammer on her house before she heard him and came out. He'd begun to wonder if he was going to have to take the damn gutter down and start over just to have something to do.

"I asked you a question."

Jack offered a shrug and a smile. "Fixing your gutter."

She propped her hands on her hips. "Why?"

"It needed doing? It's my day off, it's warm, and I didn't want to spend it indoors?"

"Well just stop it. Get down from there and go away."

"Well that's a fine way to thank a man."

"*Thank?* You want me to *thank* you? *You*, the man who thinks I'm an arsonist and a thief? If you want to know what's inside my house just come in and search it instead of crawling up there to peek in my windows."

"Peek in your windows?" If she wasn't careful, she was going to make him mad. "I don't need to peek in your windows. I've already had a guided tour through every room of your house, thanks to your kids."

Mary Jo blinked. "Every room?"

Aha. What was that that zipped through her eyes? "Every room but the one they're not allowed to go in. What do you keep in there that you don't want your own kids to see?"

"None of your business. Are you going to get down and leave, or do I call the police? This is bordering on harassment, Chief Riley."

Next door, Beth Gunnefson pulled into her driveway and waved at Mary Jo. She got out of her car. "Looks like you've got yourself a handyman," she called.

Mary Jo forced a smile. "He was just finishing. Get down from there," she added sharply, low enough that she hoped her voice didn't carry across the yard.

"Yeah." Jack climbed down the ladder and stood next to Mary Jo. "Thirsty work," he called to Beth. "Mary Jo just came out and offered me a glass of iced tea."

Mary Jo ground her teeth and forced her smile to stay in place. "Yes. It's too bad you said you couldn't—"

"You thought I meant it? Heck, I was only kidding. I never turn down a glass of iced tea. Every one of your gutters needs work. It's going to be a long day. Tea is just what I need to keep me going." He wrapped his arm around Mary Jo's shoulders and turned her toward her own front door. "See you later, Beth."

Inside, with the front door firmly closed, Mary Jo pulled away from Jack's hold and whirled on him. "Damn you. What the hell do you think you're doing?"

"Coming in for that glass of tea."

His cocky grin had her clenching her fists. She raised one and shook it in his face. "One more of your smart-mouth answers, buster, and I'm going to bop you a good one right in that grinning mouth."

Jack's smile eased and one eyebrow climbed up. "Am I making you nervous, Mary Jo?"

"You're pissing me off, Riley. Suppose you tell me just exactly what's going on here. If there's something about me you want to know, ask. If not, then get away from me and stay away."

His smile slipped again until it was only a memory. "There's a lot I want to know about you."

"Like what? Whether or not I started that fire? I didn't. Whether or not I stole those watches? That's police business, not fire department business, but I'll tell you anyway. I didn't."

"I never said you did."

"You might as well have."

Jack shook his head. "I never said anything about you setting that fire. You jumped to that conclusion all on your own. Which leads me to wonder why. Guilty conscience, Mary Jo?"

Mary Jo was so mad she couldn't get a coherent word out of her mouth.

"You had inside knowledge of the store and its contents. You knew its weaknesses. You had opportunity. And I'd have to guess that a widow with two young children to raise might have motive enough for stealing expensive jewelry."

"You've got a fertile imagination. Are you a cop, too? Am I being charged? Should I call a lawyer?"

"What went wrong, Mary Jo? Did the fire fascinate you so much that you waited too late to get out? If you'd gotten out, if your car hadn't been out front with the engine running, maybe no one would have noticed the fire for another several minutes. Plenty of time for everything in the safe to turn to ashes. Did you think then that no one would realize the watches had been stolen?"

A buzzer sounded from somewhere in the back of the house.

"Go away, Jack. I've got laundry to fold. I didn't do any of the things you're talking about." She turned to walk away.

Furious that she could walk away while he was being torn in two, one half wanting her, starting to admire and like her, the other half . . . leery, suspicious, Jack grabbed her arm and stopped her. "If you're so innocent, then tell me why you couldn't even look at my face the next morning when Dalton and I came over."

Startled, Mary Jo blinked. "What?"

"You heard me. The minute you showed your face and realized I was here you refused to so much as look at me."

"*That's* why you think I did it?" she cried. "Because I wouldn't look at you?"

"What else but a guilty conscience would change you overnight from the woman I kissed the night before, the woman who kissed me back like she meant it, the woman who laughed and joked with me the day before that?"

Mary Jo jerked free of his hold and faced him, eyes blazing, cheeks flushed. "And if I'd known who and what you were from the start, there never would have been any laughing and joking, much less kissing."

"Who and what I am?"

"You're a *firefighter*, for God's sake."

"Yeah? So?"

"So? *So?*" She flapped her arms like a bird trying to take flight. "So if I'd known you were a damn firefighter I probably never would have spoken to you in the first place. I didn't know who and what you were until you parted those damn flames like Moses parting the Red Sea and hauled me out of the fire."

"Run that by me again. I think you lost me. You wouldn't look me in the eye Saturday morning because you found out I'm a firefighter? What the hell does that have to do with anything?" Jack paused. "Oh, I get it. Arsonists don't hang with firefighters, is that it? Well, darlin', you'd be surprised what some firebugs will do."

"I'm not a firebug," she shrieked. She

marched past him and flung open the front door. "You either come up with something better than that I wouldn't look at you and have Dalton file charges, or you leave me alone. I mean it, Jack. Leave me the hell alone."

Much as he wanted to push her, drag a few answers out of her, Jack decided to back off. For now.

It was a full ten minutes before Mary Jo's hands quit shaking enough to allow her to finish folding the laundry. By then the next load was done. In the sudden quiet while the washer and dryer were both silent, she heard it again. That damn hammering, this time from the east side of the house.

The son of a bitch was still there!

Ten minutes later she heard voices. Heather and Andy were home from school and had discovered that their newest hero was at their house. The delight in their voices made her cringe.

Then she squared her shoulders. She wouldn't stand for this. She made a beeline for the telephone.

"Mother, the kids and I want to come to supper. Come get us. Right away."

"Mary Jo? What's wrong?"

"Just come get us, Mother. Now. Please. Before I commit murder."

When Arliss arrived a few minutes later Mary Jo herded the kids into her car as fast as she could, not answering their questions, not even looking in Jack Riley's direction.

The Simpson house was dark, and so was the night. The back door gave easily. Just as easily as the last time. He hadn't had time to find the watches yesterday. The woman and her brats had come home from church sooner than he'd expected. He'd thought she would have gone to her mother's but the nosey woman had come home with the rest of them.

He figured that was where she was right now, over at her mother's, but he didn't give a rat's hind end. All he cared about was finding those damn Rolex watches. They had to be here. She had to have taken them. There simply was no other possibility.

Sweat gathered inside his black leather gloves as he slipped a small, narrow beam flashlight from his pocket and made his way through the kitchen and down the hall. If he didn't find those watches soon, he was a dead man.

He had searched the downstairs carefully and thoroughly with no luck and was heading for the second floor when a bright light stabbed through the blinds on the front windows. A car pulled into the driveway.

Cursing, he barely made it out the back door

before Mary Jo Simpson and her two kids came in the front.

"This is the second time this week, Andy. You asked to be responsible for making sure the back door was locked, so I gave you that job. We have to be more careful."

"How could I?" Andy cried. "I never even came in the house after school."

Startled and chagrined, Mary Jo realized Andy was right. She had dragged him and Heather straight out of the yard and into her mother's car to escape Jack Riley. Andy couldn't have left the door open.

"You're right," she told him. "I'm sorry. I must have done it myself."

But she hadn't. She knew she hadn't.

Later that night, enclosed in the room that Andy and Heather were not allowed to enter, a new color appeared on Mary Jo's canvas. Pale blue. For fear.

Someone had been in her house while she'd been gone.

# FIVE

The *Two Oaks Weekly Register* hit the local newsstands and mail boxes Thursday. Mary Jo wondered if it was possible for a person to die of humiliation.

There it was, in black and white, covering almost the entire front page. The photo of her and Jack kissing on the sidewalk while the volunteer firefighters fought the fire in the store in the background.

She had barely unfolded her copy when she got a call from her good friend Rachel Morgan in Oklahoma City.

"What's going on out there in the Texas Panhandle?"

"Well." Mary Jo laughed. "It's great talking to you too. I've been fine. And you?"

"Mary Jo, when Jared finds a story about you on the AP, complete with photographs . . ."

"You're kidding! Associated Press?"

"The one and only. How else would an Oklahoma City television station get a picture of you being ravished by some macho firefighter?"

Mary Jo groaned. Jared Morgan was the general manager of an Oklahoma City television station. If his station had the story and photographs, she supposed she was going to have to call the Simpsons before they called her.

"So who's the hunk?" Rachel asked.

Mary Jo reluctantly told the entire tale. Rachel made her laugh at not only herself, but the situation. "God, I'm glad you called," she told her friend. "I've missed you."

"So come see us."

"Maybe this summer," Mary Jo said, "when the kids are out of school."

She and Rachel talked for several more minutes, then said good-bye.

Next came the local calls. After the first three from friends teasing her about the photograph, Mary Jo took her phone off the hook. She wouldn't have stuck her nose out of the house the rest of the week if the kids hadn't polished off the last of the milk at breakfast Friday morning.

She should have known she would run into Jack on the dairy aisle. The man was *everywhere*. As she turned to go the other way without speaking to him, the store manager spotted them while he was sweeping at the end of the aisle.

"Hey, our hero and the damsel he rescued. How about another kiss? I could take a picture of you in front of the eggs, put the eggs on sale, and make a bundle."

Jack grinned. "Sounds fine to me. How 'bout it, Mary Jo?"

"How about if the both of you get a life?" She picked up a gallon of milk and made her way past Jack to the checkout stand. Luck was not with her. There was only one checker on duty, and she was just starting to unload Dorothy Bannister's full cart.

Naturally, Jack followed Mary Jo and stood in line behind her. The manager followed them with his broom. "So what's doin' down at the firehouse, Jack?"

Jack hefted the three pounds of cheese he'd picked up on the dairy aisle. "It's chili night. You coming?"

Whenever the fire department needed a little extra money, the volunteer firefighters cooked up a big batch of chili and invited the whole town to stop by and indulge themselves, for five dollars a head. Most of the ingredients were donated by local business, the rest purchased by individuals.

"What do you need money for this time?" the grocer asked.

"Pagers."

"Yeah? For you and the volunteers?"

"Yep. That way we're never out of reach."

"Hey, good idea. Count me in."

Jack grinned. "We already did. Who do you think donated the beans and bread?"

The manager's lips twitched. "Let me guess. My wife."

"You be sure and thank her."

"Yeah." The grocer laughed. "Guess I better come on down. Sounds like she won't be cooking my dinner tonight. How 'bout you, Mary Jo?" As he swept past with his broom he winked at her. She was getting damn tired of being winked at. "You having chili at the firehouse tonight?"

"I'm afraid I have other plans," she offered with feigned regret.

"Coward," Jack whispered in her ear.


"But Mom, the whole town will be there."

"Not the whole town," Mary Jo told her son. He'd been whining since he and Heather had come home from school. Chief Jack had stopped by the school during the day and invited the teachers and students to the chili supper, and Andy had his heart set on going.

"But Chief Jack will be there," Heather added.

*That*, Mary Jo thought with a rush of anger, *is the reason we're not going.*

"Are you mad at Chief Jack?" Andy asked.

"What makes you say that?"

Andy shrugged and stared at the grungy laces

of his running shoes. "I don't know. You wouldn't let us stay and talk to him when he was fixin' the gutters. Now you won't go to the fire-house for chili. And they need the money, Mom. Everybody says so."

"We'll send a donation."

"But Mo-om."

"Do you have homework?"

"Ah, Mom."


Andy thought about it all night and figured that Mom must be mad at Jack for something, and he didn't know what to do about it. Jack, Andy had decided, would make a great dad. Andy was tired of not having a dad.

Mom was cool, and she pitched great, not like a girl at all, but it wasn't the same as having a dad.

But how could Jack be their new dad if Mom wouldn't go see him, or invite him over, or stay and visit when Jack was there?

Who understood grownups anyway?

Okay, if Mom wouldn't go see Jack at the firehouse, then Andy just had to figure out a way to get Jack to come see Mom at home.

And he knew just how to do it.

Saturday morning instead of watching cartoons, he talked Heather into playing in the backyard with him. For his plan to work, Heather had to help.

"But what if we get caught?"

"That's such a *girl* thing, worrying about getting caught. You want Jack to be our new dad, don't you?"

Heather did. Very much. He was big and strong and smiled at her. "Okay, what do I have to do?"

Andy pulled the matchbook from his pocket. He'd found it in the junk drawer in the kitchen. He planned to put it back in just a little while.

"First you gotta make sure Mom's got her hair combed. Maybe get her to put on some foo-foo water, lipstick. You know, girl stuff."

"But when do I tell her to call Jack?"

"Just keep an eye on that pile of leaves. You'll know when it's time."

Mary Jo put eggs on to boil for the tuna salad she planned to make for lunch later. She checked the setting on the burner, then turned away and saw Heather come in from the backyard.

"Having fun, sweetie?"

"I guess." Heather peered at her, tilting her head first one way then the other.

"What are you looking at?"

"Your hair." Heather smiled. "Can I comb it?"

Mary Jo bit back a laugh. It must look pretty bad if her six-year-old thought it needed combing. But she and Heather rarely had the time to spend alone together doing girl things, so Mary Jo nodded. "Sure. Let's go up to my room and I'll sit at the dresser."

Heather paused and peered over her shoulder out the back door.

"What's Andy doing?" Mary Jo asked.

Heather turned back and smiled again. "Playing." Then she took her mother's hand and skipped through the house to the stairs. Upstairs Mary Jo sat on the stool before her dresser and let Heather comb her hair for her. Then they started on makeup, with Heather in charge. Experimenting, and with much giggling, they painted each other's faces. Bright, rosy cheeks, gobs of eye makeup, and horridly vivid lipstick.

"Now perfume," Heather insisted.

"Okay. One squirt for you, one for me."

"Two. You need two, Mommy."

As Mary Jo conceded and gave her neck an extra spritz of cologne they heard a shout from the backyard.

With a startled look, Heather dashed to the window. "Oh, Mommy. You need to call Chief Jack."

"Whatever for?"

"Because the backyard's on fire."


The damage was minimal, except for Mary Jo's nerves. A ten-foot circle of scorched earth in her backyard, and a nine-year-old boy with a great deal of explaining to do.

The sirens, not to mention the fifteen-foot flames, drew neighbors like a magnet. To protect their yards, Mary Jo's immediate neighobors rushed for garden hoses long stored for the winter in sheds or garages and were none too happy about having to do it.

From down the block, twelve-year-old Janie Martin, the younger sister of Pam, who often babysat Andy and Heather, rushed over on Rollerblades. With her ever present camera she took snapshots of the fire, firefighters, and eveyone else.

Mary Jo groaned. Janie was out to become a photojournalist. Dollars to donuts, she'd take those shots down to the paper and try to sell them. After the shot that made the front page last week, Mary Jo didn't doubt that a fire in her own backyard would surely make the news.

"Hell, darlin'." Jack swiped his forearm across his face to get rid of some of the water. "If you'd wanted to see me, you could have just invited me over."

"That's lame, Riley."

"What's the matter? Did you just not like that patch of grass? Or does everything around you go up in flames? What were you doing, by the way, trying out new makeup?"

It took Mary Jo a minute to realize what Jack was talking about. She'd come straight from her makeup session with Heather. She and Heather both looked like a couple of painted Kewpie dolls. Mary Jo refused to be embarrassed for playing with her daughter. "Don't start on me. I'm not in the habit of setting my own yard on fire, or anything else, for that matter."

"Well it looks to me like somebody had themselves a high old time, with the makeup—looks cute on you, by the way—and playing with matches. Until things got out of hand."

Mary Jo felt the blood drain from her face. "Matches?"

Jack pulled a half-used book of matches from his pocket. "Found them in the flower bed."

Mary Jo swallowed hard. She recognized them. They were from a steak house in Oklahoma City. She kept them in the junk drawer in the kitchen. Standing there staring at them, feeling Jack stare at her, she was sure she felt her blood pressure rising.

"Andy," she called, striving for calm.

"He's in the house, Mommy."

Mary Jo looked down and saw that Heather had come to stand beside her. "Go get him for me, will you?"

"You're not gonna yell at him for starting the fire, are you?"

"You both know you're not to play with matches. Somebody could have been hurt."

"He only did it so you would have to ask Chief Jack to come over."

Mary Jo had to clear her throat twice before she could speak. "What did you say?"

"Well, last time there was a fire, Chief Jack kissed you. It was in the paper and everything."

Beside Mary Jo, Jack made a strangling sound. Mary Jo shot him a murderous look.

"Andy thought maybe you were mad at Chief Jack, since you wouldn't take us to eat chili at the firehouse last night. He said if we had a fire then you'd have to ask Chief Jack to come over, and maybe he'd kiss you again, and if he thought you were a good enough kisser, maybe he'd want to marry you and be our new daddy. Andy thinks Chief Jack would make a good daddy for us. Don't you, Mommy?"

From that point, things got worse. Three firefighters and two neighbors burst out laughing.

Heather frowned. "Did I say something funny?"

"No, sweetie." Mary Jo turned Heather toward the house. "Go inside now and wash your face."

When Mary Jo turned back toward Jack, ready to . . . to . . . She didn't know what she was going to do. She never got the chance to find out. That he was blushing at the ribbing from his friends was surprising enough. That he would fall in with them was too much. He grabbed her and kissed her, and Janie Martin took a picture.

It made the front page of the next edition of

the *Two Oaks Weekly Register*. Right along with the story of how and why the fire in her backyard occurred.

In a house across town, a man looked at the latest photograph of Mary Jo and Jack and took another slug of Maalox. Was Riley in on it with her?

Nah, he was too upright, the prig. Word had it that he even thought maybe Mary Jo had set that fire at the jewelry store. Let him think that. That was fine. Great, in fact. Everything was great. Except he still hadn't found the watches.

He'd planned it so carefully, timed out every second. Everything would work. All he'd had to do was slip in the back door, take the watches that had just come in, and set the fire to cover the theft.

He'd gone in the back door as planned. Sweating, heart pounding, he'd slipped down the hall into the office where the safe was. But the damn watches weren't there.

He hadn't known what else to do but go ahead and set the fire. If Mary Jo had the watches, he would get them from her. That had been the plan that had loosely formed in his mind as he'd struck the match.

Damn the woman. Who would have thought Arliss and Tom Kelley's little girl would take a thing in the world that didn't belong to her?

She had to have them.

"And I have to get them," he muttered.

The threats were coming faster now. They would kill him if he didn't come up with the money he owed them.

Kill him twice, he thought with a nervous chuckle. His old college buddy on one side, who'd set up the deal with the watches, and the syndicate—the one he owed so damn much money to—on the other.

It had started out simply enough. A few side bets at the track over in Ruidoso. In one weekend he'd made more money than he knew what to do with. Why the hell hadn't he quit while he'd been ahead?

But no, he'd had to go and bet it all, lose it all. Then he'd had to go and accept the offer to try to win it back, on borrowed money. Damn his hide, he knew better, but he'd been so *sure* he could win it back.

Now he owed so much money it was scary. Almost as scary as the people he owed it to. And they were getting impatient.

So he'd worked out this deal to steal the watches. That was supposed to take care of everything and leave him with a little pocket change to get him back in the game at the start of the next racing season.

Except Mary Jo Simpson had beaten him to the watches. If he didn't get them back it was a toss-up as to who would kill him first.

⊰———————⊱

Andy was grounded for two weeks. No friends, no television, no Nintendo.

The only good thing to happen all week was that Mary Jo finally got her car replaced. Tuesday morning her mother drove her to Amarillo, where she picked out one just like the one that had been totaled. Except this time she was able to get a four-door.

The day the paper came out, Mary Jo took her phone off the hook again. Because he couldn't reach her by phone all evening, Jack went to her house the next day.

"I'm not speaking to you." Mary Jo moved to shut the door in his face.

Jack braced it with a hand and a foot. "Just thought I'd check to see if anything was on fire."

"If that's supposed to be funny—"

"Sorry. Are you going to invite me in?"

"Only in your dreams, mister."

In his dreams. That was the problem, Jack admitted silently. She was in his dreams. Every night. Every day. And he couldn't get her out. It was driving him crazy. His gut was still telling him she was innocent, his brain still screaming warnings. He wanted it settled. He needed to make up his mind about her once and for all.

"You never did answer my question from last week," he told her. "I need an answer, Mary Jo."

"What question?"

"Let me in."

"No."

"What do you keep in that private room of yours that you won't let your kids see?"

"Oh, for crying out loud. I keep dead bodies."

"Let me in, Mary Jo. Talk to me. Convince me."

Mary Jo propped her hands on her hips. "Whatever happened to 'innocent until proven guilty'?"

"Do you *want* me to think you set that fire?"

"It doesn't seem to matter what I want. You've already made up your mind."

Jack stood before her and stuffed his hands in the pockets of his jacket to keep from reaching for her. Damn, but he wanted to touch her. And that was just plain crazy. "No. I haven't. Help me do that. Answer my question. Look at you. Even now you have trouble looking me in the eye. Talk to me, Mary Jo."

Mary Jo met his gaze squarely. "I did not take the watches. I did not start the fire."

Dammit, he believed her. He had no business believing her. Hadn't he learned that lesson the hard way in Dallas?

"Then tell me," he said quietly, "why wouldn't you look at me the morning after the fire."

"Is that what this is about?" she cried, flinging her hands up in frustration. "Your ego took a beating because a woman didn't fall all over you?"

"Dammit, this has nothing to do with my ego. You have to admit there was something there when I kissed you that night."

"I don't have to admit anything."

"You kissed me back."

"I was glad to be alive. I would have kissed a goat if it had gotten me out of that fire."

Jack frowned, nodded. "Okay. I can buy that. So why wouldn't you look at me the next morning?"

"Why does it matter?"

"Because you keep evading the question. It's my job to help find out who set that fire. The jewelry is Dalton's business. When a woman who's been flirting with me gets pulled from a fire and then can't look me in the face, I get suspicious."

"I was not flirting with you."

"Yes you were, and you were good enough to get me interested."

"You're the one who brought up that stupid joke about having an affair."

He cocked his head. "Who says I was joking?"

"Like I said, Riley. In your dreams."

"Dammit, Mary Jo, why won't you answer my question?"

Suddenly Mary Jo was tired of arguing, tired

of evading his question. "I told you. You're a firefighter."

"What does that have to do with why you wouldn't look at me?"

Mary Jo steeled herself. "Come with me."

As she led him into the living room, Jack paused. "What's that beeping noise?"

"The phone." She pulled the receiver out from beneath the sofa cushion and placed it back in its cradle on the end table.

"No wonder I couldn't get through."

"There's the answer to your question." Mary Jo pointed to the flags on the mantel. Anger flushed in her cheeks. "Every man in my life has died in the line of duty to other people, Jack."

"And that makes you angry."

"You're damn right it does. I won't have anything to do with a man with a job like yours."

"For somebody who doesn't like public servants, you sure do seem to need rescuing often enough. We're good enough to call on for help, but not good enough for anything else? Is that it?"

"It has nothing to do with being good enough," she cried. "It has to do with men risking their lives for everyone else but their own family. Getting themselves killed and leaving their families to fend for themselves."

"And that makes you angry."

"You're damn right it does. Jeff was supposed to get married, have babies, grow old. Daddy was supposed to spend his retirement years fishing and bouncing grandchildren on his knees. Al was going to teach Andy to play baseball. Now I have to do it, and I'm no good at it. We wanted another baby. There won't be any more babies for me. None of that will happen. We've all been cheated out of what we could have had because three otherwise sensible men went off and got themselves killed in the line of duty. Yes. It makes me angry."

Jack was starting to feel a bit of his own anger at her attitude. "Did it ever occur to you that it was their own families they were thinking of that made them do the things they did? I knew your brother. Not well, but I knew him. Jeff hated anything that hinted at injustice. He was always taking up for the little guy, the underdog, but there was more to it than that. Like a million other guys who volunteer to serve their country, he wanted to make sure that his family was always safe. That his family never had to live the way people are forced to live in so many other countries. And he didn't believe in leaving the security of his family up to somebody else. Your dad was the same way. I didn't know your husband, but I'd bet my right arm that he was just like them."

Shaken by Jack's words, Mary Jo once again could not look him in the eye. "What makes you say that? About Al, I mean."

"Because I don't think you could love and

marry a man who let someone else do his fighting for him. A man who left the safety and security of his family, and yeah, his friends and neighbors, up to somebody else."

"You don't know anything about me."

"You're wrong about that. I know how you were raised, because it's the same way your brother Jeff was raised. The same way my brother and I were raised. The same way half the people in this town were raised."

"It doesn't make any difference," Mary Jo told him. "I won't have anything to do with a man with a dangerous job, and yours is one of the most dangerous I know of."

Jack was quiet a minute as he studied her face. "I think I'm flattered."

That was the last thing Mary Jo expected him to say. She looked at him in surprise.

"I guess that means I wasn't the only one feeling something here."

Mary Jo looked away again quickly. "I don't know what you're talking about."

"Don't you? You must have felt some of what I was feeling when we first met. Call it . . . attraction. Maybe just the possibility of attraction. But it was there, and you were feeling it, or my being a firefighter wouldn't have made any difference."

"And because I wouldn't look at you the morning after the fire, you decided that meant I had something to hide."

Jack sighed. "I . . . yeah. I guess that's about it."

"Do you always jump to conclusions that way? Don't you have any objectivity at all when it comes to arson investigation?"

Jack smiled ruefully. "I used to. Hell, Mary Jo, we're a fine pair, you and me."

"We're not a pair."

"No. I guess we're not. And that's a damn shame. I think we could have been great together. But you see, you're not the only one here with hangups."

"Let me guess." Mary Jo smiled sweetly and batted her lashes. "Your ego got bruised when I didn't fall all over you."

Jack let out a harsh laugh. "Darlin', if you had fallen all over me before the fire, I would have been right back all over you. If you'd done it after the fire, after I realized the fire was no accident, I would have run as far and fast from you as I could have gotten. I don't believe you set that fire, Mary Jo. I never did."

Mary Jo blinked. "Then . . . why all of this . . . this—"

"The truth is, I thought you knew the day you wrecked your car that I was a firefighter. My name and picture have been in the local paper enough, I'm used to people knowing who I am and what I do. I thought . . . I guess I thought that was part of why you were attracted to me."

"I never said I was—"

"You didn't have to say it. Your eyes said it for you. That, and the way you kissed me back. Grandma what's her name was wrong, by the way. Not all your juices have dried up."

"Jack, why are we having this conversation? And you leave my juices out of it."

Jack let out a breath. "Look, the last woman I felt an instant attraction to turned out to be using me, because I was a firefighter, to get her kicks. She used to ask me all about every fire I got called out on. Then she started showing up at fire scenes when they were announced on the news. I was young enough and gullible enough to be flattered. I thought she'd come to watch me play the big, bad fireman."

Despite herself, Mary Jo was interested. "And?"

"And." He took a deep breath, looked away, and let it out. "And, it turned out she was the one setting the fires."

Mary Jo winced. "Ouch."

"Yeah. Ouch."

She shook her head. "So because you thought I was attracted to you—"

"There was no thinking to it, darlin'. You were, and you still are."

"You wish," she tossed back. "You figured if I was attracted to you, it must be because I was going to get my kicks by setting fires and watching you run around putting them out?"

Put that way, Jack had to admit it sounded stupid.

"That's lame, Jack. Really lame."

"No more lame than you assuming I'm going to get myself killed just to disappoint you."

The entire conversation was so . . . bizarre. Mary Jo finally gave up trying to make sense out of herself or Jack. She chuckled. "You were right. We are a pair. A pair of screwed up idiots."

Jack reached out and stroked a finger across her check, sending sparks of fire spiraling down to the pit of her stomach.

"I'd like to pair up with you, Mary Jo Simpson, just to see what would happen."

Mary Jo's smile faded. "I'm not into experiments or one-night stands."

"No. You're not the type. Neither am I. But I'm not the type to just walk away from whatever it is you do to me when I'm with you."

Heat stung Mary Jo's cheeks. Her mouth went dry. "What I do to you?"

"Face it." He gave her that cocky grin that curled her toes. "When we kiss, it's spontaneous combustion, darlin'."

"Jack—"

The phone rang. Mary Jo had never been so grateful for an interruption in her life. She didn't have a clue as to what she'd been about to say. She grabbed the receiver as though it were a lifeline. "Hello?"

She thought she heard someone mumble, but

the line was full of static. "Hello? You'll have to speak up. I can't hear you."

*Please speak up. I'm not ready to face Jack again just yet. Come on, whoever you are, keep me on the phone.*

"Think you're clever, don't you?"

It was a man, but she didn't recognize the voice. It sounded muffled, as though he were trying to talk around a mouthful of mush. "Who is this? What are you talking about?"

"I'm talking about you beating me to the goods, lady. They're supposed to be mine. I want them."

A chill skittered down Mary Jo's spine. "What—" Her mouth was suddenly so dry she could barely speak. "What are you talking about?"

Jack couldn't hear what the caller was saying, but he saw the blood drain from Mary Jo's face. He stepped closer.

"But I don't . . . I didn't . . . I don't have them," she insisted, her eyes turning dark. "No! If you—" Slowly she pulled the phone from her ear and hung it up. Her hand was shaking badly.

"Mary Jo? What's wrong? Who was that?"

Mary Jo looked at Jack with eyes huge and haunted. "He wants the watches."

"Who?" Jack demanded.

Mary Jo shook her head. "I don't know. His voice was . . . muffled. I didn't recognize it."

"What did he say?"

Mary Jo shuddered. "He said if I didn't give him the watches, something would hap—" She swayed.

Jack caught her shoulders to steady her. "Something would what?"

"Something would happen . . . to my children."

Jack swore and reached for the phone.

"No!" Mary Jo jerked the phone from his hand. "Who are you calling?"

"I'm calling Dalton."

"No." She shook her head. "He was emphatic about that. If I tell the police, he said he would know, and . . . and he'd hurt one of my kids."

"You told him you didn't have the watches?"

She nodded. "He didn't believe me."

"What are you supposed to do? What else did he say?"

"I'm supposed to wait for him to call back with instructions on where to leave the watches. Oh, God." She sank to the sofa and buried her face in her hands. "What am I going to do? This sounds like something out of a bad movie."

If there had been any lingering doubt in Jack's mind about Mary Jo's innocence, the devastation on her face killed it. She'd been telling him the truth all along. She hadn't set the fire or robbed the store. His own insecurities had tried to blame her. He swore at himself for not trusting his gut. He swore at the bastard on the phone for putting that look of terror in Mary Jo's eyes.

"All right." Jack knelt before Mary Jo and took her face in his hands. "Look at me. Here's what we're going to do."

"*We're* not going to do anything," Mary Jo said, her voice gaining strength. "This is my problem, not yours. For all you know, I have those watches upstairs in my secret room right this minute."

"No," he said, staring her in the eye. "You don't have them. And if you think I'm going to leave you to deal with this alone, then think again, darlin'. I'm not budging."

# SIX

Jack didn't budge.

Neither did he waste time. The first thing he did was have Mary Jo call the phone company and order Caller ID and Trace added to her phone line immediately.

After that Mary Jo drove to the school and spoke personally with the principal and all of Andy and Heather's teachers. Without going into detail, she made certain they understood that Andy and Heather were to leave the school with no one—*no one*—other than her, her mother, or Jack.

Her actions would start talk, Mary Jo knew, but that was all right. If people thought Andy and Heather might be in danger, they would be more inclined to keep an eye on them.

But that single arrangement wasn't good enough, as far as Mary Jo was concerned. "I was married to a cop for too many years," she told Jack. "I know what can happen. I won't take any chances."

She called her mother, who agreed to take Andy and Heather to visit Al's parents in Oklahoma for the weekend. Since it was Friday, they would leave that very afternoon.

Mary Jo picked them up when school was out and took them home to pack. They were ecstatic at the idea of getting to see their other grandparents.

Mary Jo had been right that talk would start. No sooner had her mother left town with the children than Dalton called. When Mary Jo recognized his voice, she nearly strangled on the words to tell him what was happening. But she couldn't tell him. She wouldn't take that chance. Not with her children.

"Oh, hi, Dalton," she managed to say in a semi-normal tone. "You must be looking for Jack. Hang on."

"Jack? No, I was call—"

Mary Jo didn't wait for him to say he was calling her. She thrust the phone at Jack, begging him with her eyes not to say anything.

Jack took the phone. "Hey, what's up?"

"Suppose you tell me," Dalton said.

"There any law against a guy finally talking a woman into fixing supper for him?"

"Supper, huh?"

"Yeah, and it smells so good my mouth's watering."

"You sure there's nothing going on there I should know about?"

"Now, Dalton, I'm not the type to kiss and tell. My momma raised me to be a gentleman."

"Is that a fact? So tell me, how are Mary Jo's kids?"

"Andy and Heather?" When he spoke their names, panic registered in Mary Jo's eyes. "What about them?"

"You're not going to tell me what's going on, are you?"

"Not just now, no."

"Just tell me this much, Jack. Are any laws being broken that I should know about?"

"Not by anybody I know. I'm coming, Mary Jo," he called, as though Mary Jo was in the other room. "My supper's ready. Gotta go, Dalton. Talk to you later."

When Jack hung up the phone, Mary Jo sagged. "He knows something."

"He was fishing."

"Why?"

"Probably because of your visit to the school. When a mother gives instructions like that it usually means somebody's after the kids."

"I know. But I couldn't help it. It had to be done."

"I know." Jack turned her away from him

and rubbed her shoulders. "You did what you had to do."

His hands on her shoulders were warm and worked magic. Mary Jo felt some of her tension ease. Maybe a little too much for comfort. She shrugged away from his touch and turned toward him. "I guess I better start making good on what you told Dalton. How does spaghetti sound?"

"So tell me," Mary Jo said as she passed a slice of garlic toast to Jack. "What's your other job besides being fire chief?"

"I don't have another job."

"You're a full-time volunteer?"

"You trying to find out if I can afford to take you out?"

"I'm trying to make conversation."

"Fire Chief is a paid position."

"Since when? I thought all the local firefighters were volunteers."

"All but the chief, since two years ago."

"You mean since the bomb at the newspaper?"

"Yeah. After that, the volunteer fire chief got transferred on his real job and the town decided to hire somebody with experience."

"Namely, you."

"Namely me. I'm sorry you don't like my job."

Mary Jo shook her head and looked down at

her plate. "It's not that I don't appreciate what you do. I just can't live with it, that's all."

"So it's like I said. It's okay to use me when you need me for a fire emergency, but other than that you've got no use for me, is that it?"

"Don't put words in my mouth, Jack. And don't presume to think you know what I think."

"Then suppose you tell me what you think?"

"About what?"

"About us."

Mary Jo looked down at her plate. "There is no us."

"Isn't there?"

"No."

Jack toyed with his fork and taunted her. "Want me to kiss you again to prove you wrong?"

That got her to look at him, albeit with fire in her eyes. "You come near me with kissing on your mind and you'll get a plate of spaghetti in the face for your troubles."

At his waist Jack felt his new pager go off. "Damn."

"What?"

"My pager." He unhooked it from his belt to read the message.

"I didn't hear it go off."

Jack wiggled his eyebrows. "It vibrates."

"I guess the chili fund-raiser must have been successful." Mary Jo swallowed hard. "Is it a fire?"

Jack frowned as he read the message. "Wreck. A semi and a pickup out west of town." He pushed back from the table and stood.

"You have to leave," she said dully. Her tone surprised her. She should want him to leave, but she didn't. And that worried her.

"It's part of that job you hate."

"I don't hate the job, or the man," she added, looking up at him.

"Good. That's . . . good." Jack rounded the table slowly. "I don't know if I'll make it back tonight. Lock every door and window in this house. Leave the lights on. And if he calls back, record it on your answering machine."

Mary Jo grimaced. "I've already thought of that. I'm not completely helpless."

"I know. And Mary Jo?" Standing beside her chair, he waited until she tilted her head up to look at him. When she did, he leaned down and brushed his lips across hers.

Her soft intake of breath prompted him to press for more, so he went with it, taking her mouth with his, letting his eyes slide shut so he could savor the taste of her. Garlic, sauce, and a deeper flavor, sweet, that was hers alone.

When his breath starting coming faster Jack knew he had to back away. Doing so took considerably more effort than he'd anticipated.

Mary Jo blinked up at him. "What was that for?"

"That," he said softly, "was for us."

"I told you, there is no us."

"You're wrong, Mary Jo. There is most definitely an us."


Fear kept Mary Jo awake until sunup. Fear of the unknown caller who threatened her and her children because he thought she had something she didn't have. Fear of what he might do when he realized she really didn't have the missing watches.

Fear for Jack. Working a traffic accident couldn't be anywhere near as dangerous as rushing into a burning building, so she assumed he was relatively safe. But still, there was fear. A car's gas tank could ignite. A truck could roll over on rescue workers. There could be another downed power line, she thought with a shiver. Yes, there was fear for Jack.

And there was that other fear, brought on by Jack's kiss and his parting comment.

*There is most definitely an us.*

There wasn't. There couldn't be.

And yet . . . when he kissed her she could almost believe him. She didn't recall ever being so affected by a mere kiss before. Her reactions, the feelings that rushed through her when their lips were touching, were scarier than anything she'd ever experienced, short of facing the rest of her life alone.

She was afraid, so very much afraid, that she was falling for Jack Riley.

Sometime around sunup she dozed, but woke with a start when the phone rang at 7:30. She grabbed for it. "Hello?"

"It's a good thing it's me. You were supposed to let the answering machine get it."

"Jack." Mary Jo let out a long breath of relief. "It's you."

"I'm coming over. In case your caller decides to drive by your house now and then, there's no sense letting him see my pickup, so I'm walking."

"There's no need—"

"I'll be there in ten minutes."

The line went dead.

Jack was as good as his word. Mary Jo scarcely had time to splash water on her face and pull on a pair of jeans and a sweatshirt before the doorbell rang. She was awake enough to make sure it was Jack before she opened the door, but that was about it.

He came in on a breath of cold morning air. "You look like hell."

"Ah, those lovely words that every woman longs to hear first thing in the morning when she's had about an hour's sleep."

Jack stepped inside and closed the door and locked it behind him. With one thumb he traced a dark circle beneath one of her eyes. "Couldn't sleep?" he asked softly.

Mary Jo grimaced. "How can you tell?"

There may have been shadows under her eyes, but Jack's shadows were *in* his eyes. Mary Jo fought the urge to cup his face in her hands. "How did your night go?"

"Not nearly as well as my morning."

Mary Jo saw it coming this time. He was going to kiss her. And she wasn't going to stop him. She wanted it, she admitted to herself. Wanted the taste of him, wanted the heat in her blood, wanted to feel her head spin and her knees go weak and the world fall away at her feet.

The instant his lips touched hers, all of those things and more happened inside Mary Jo. Yes, she was very much afraid she was falling for Jack Riley.

Jack wasn't in much better shape himself. He'd been thinking about her all night while he worked the accident out on the highway, and later, back at the firehouse when he and the crew had cleaned the equipment and readied it for the next emergency.

He wanted her. He wanted to touch, to taste. He wanted to lose himself in her for a while. Most of all, he wanted to trust her. He wanted someone to trust with his feelings, his heart, and he wondered if she was the one.

He slid his arms around her and pulled her close, liking, very much, the way her curves fit against him. She was firm with muscle, soft in all the right places to make his blood heat. And heat it did.

No garlic this morning, he thought as his tongue slid against hers. Mint. And Mary Jo. Pure, sweet, Mary Jo. A man could get lost here and never care. She was his. He could feel it in the way she suddenly wrapped her arms around him, the way her lips gave, the way her body accommodated his. The way she made that little sound in the back of her throat. The sound of surrender.

He could have her right there and then.

She was lost. Mary Jo knew she was lost to this man and the magic he made inside her. It was scary and glorious, dark and bright. Right. And . . . too soon.

"Jack." Her voice was breathless as she twisted her mouth free. Good Lord, she was gasping. And she had her arms around him. How had that happened?

Jack ran his hands up her back, liking the feel of her, not ready to let go. He was hard and aching, and she had to know, the way she was pressed up against him.

But when he saw the fatigue in her eyes he knew now wasn't the time to take their relationship that next big step. "Why don't you go back to bed and get some sleep?"

More rattled than she cared to let on, Mary Jo stepped away and smoothed her hair back with both hands. "I'm awake now. And I'm hungry."

"Good." He grinned. "What's for breakfast? I haven't eaten all night."

"I fixed your supper last night, now you expect breakfast?"

Jack shrugged. Slipping an arm around her shoulders, he turned her toward the kitchen. "If you've got eggs, I'll cook."

"This could be interesting."

"Don't you know that all firefighters are great cooks?"

"No. That must have slipped past me somehow. Is it a job requirement?"

"In a regular fire department we work twenty-four-hour shifts. It's cook, or starve."

"So why aren't you working?"

"Two Oaks is not a regular fire department. As long as we get the job done, the town fathers pretty much leave me alone."

"How convenient."

"I think so."

Jack fixed omelets with cheese, bacon, and bell peppers, and Mary Jo made coffee. While they ate she asked him about the accident he'd been called out on the night before.

Jack shook his head. "You don't want to hear about it."

Something in his voice gave her pause, and maybe explained those shadows in his eyes. "Was it bad?"

"It was bad," he said tersely.

Mary Jo picked up her coffee and took a sip. Firefighters, she figured, must be like cops. They didn't want to bring the ugly part of their job home with them. They didn't think anyone who didn't do the job would understand, and they didn't want their loved ones exposed to the ugliness, didn't want them to know of the danger.

Not that she qualified as one of Jack's loved ones.

Not that she wanted to.

They wouldn't admit, even to themselves, these macho men, that they needed someone to talk to, someone they could trust with their feelings, their fears, their pain. A cop thought only another cop would understand. Firefighters, she assumed, must be the same. Mary Jo swore.

Jack blinked. "Pardon?"

"Cops. Firefighters," she said with disgust. "You guys are all alike."

"What's that supposed to mean?"

"I was married to a cop. Al never would talk about the bad parts of his job to me. It really used to make me angry the way he would bottle everything up because he thought he knew best what I should and should not hear. From the look in your eyes and the set of your jaw, I guess firefighters are just as bad."

Jack stared at her for a long, silent moment before he spoke. "Does it matter?"

Mary Jo hesitated. Her answer, she knew,

would tell him more than the words themselves. She told herself to tell him no. It didn't matter. It couldn't matter, because they were only friends. Not even that. Acquaintances, that was all. A mere acquaintance wouldn't care how Jack's job affected him or what put those shadows in his eyes.

"Yes." Her voice shook. "I think it matters."

Her answer shot through Jack like lightning. If what happened on his job mattered to her, then *he* must matter, a least a little.

"Never mind," she said. "I can see you're not going to tell me anything. Forget I asked. You're another one of those strong, silent types. A dangerous job, and won't talk. That's two strikes, Jack."

"How many do I get?"

"One. Maybe."

"I won't quit my job, Mary Jo."

"I'm not asking you to."

"Glad to hear it."

"This is crazy." Frustrated, with herself and with him, Mary Jo rose and started cleaning up. "You're still who you are. That's not going to change."

"And you don't like who I am?"

She stood at the sink with her back to him. "I didn't say that. It's just that who you are and what you do are so closely tied."

"They are," Jack admitted. "I guess that's

not ever going to change. As long as I have the ability and the skill to put out fires, save property, save lives, then I'll do it."

Mary Jo hung her head and stared down the drain. "I know," she said quietly.

"You know. But can you accept it? Accept me?"

"What—" She stopped and cleared her throat. "What do you mean?"

Jack rose and stood behind her, not touching her, but wanting to, badly. "You know what I mean." He was so close that his breath stirred the scent in her hair. He closed his eyes and breathed it in. "I want to make love with you."

Heat flushed through Mary Jo at his words. Heat, and weakness. And need. Oh, Lord, the need. It settled in her belly like a lump of hot steel.

"You're tired, Mary Jo. Go back to bed. We'll talk later."

If he hadn't said that, Mary Jo was very much afraid she would have turned and thrown herself at him.

But he did say it, and he was right. She was too tired to think straight. She didn't want to look back later and regret whatever it was that might happen between her and Jack. He'd offered her a reprieve, and she took it.

❖――――――❖

Jack was still cursing himself three hours later. "When did I get to be such a noble bastard?"

When, indeed. Twice this morning she'd been his for the taking. Twice he'd deliberately given her the out he knew she'd needed.

But dammit, this was too important to risk messing up. He didn't just want her. He *wanted* her. Wanted to see if they could build something together.

What that something was, he wasn't sure, and feared that if he knew, if he could see the future, he might turn tail and run. Falling for a woman like Mary Jo Simpson was scary business.

*Falling for?*

Yeah. Okay. There. He'd said it. Sort of. He was falling for Mary Jo Simpson. Falling hard.

He didn't want to rush her into something she might regret. He didn't want regrets, not hers, not his. So he wouldn't rush her. He would give her time to come to terms with what was happening between them. What would happen.

Then there were her kids to consider. If he and Mary Jo were to have something good and strong, Andy and Heather would be affected, would be a part of whatever developed.

Every time he thought of Heather's explanation of why Andy had set the fire in the backyard, Jack got a funny feeling in the region of his heart. He thought it might be love. Or fear. Maybe both. God, what a rush, to have a boy go to that much trouble to get his mom and the man he thought of as a hero together.

"Hell, Andy," he muttered. "I'm no damn hero. I'm just a man."

But he'd like to be Andy's hero, and Heather's. And most of all he'd like to be the man their mother wanted to share herself with.

She said she didn't want anything to do with a man with a dangerous job. Looking at the flags on her mantel, he could understand that. But the flags also told him that she admired the kind of man who took up for those who couldn't help themselves, a man who stood for law and order, a man willing to fight for what he believed in.

"That's not me," he muttered. He didn't see himself as that kind of man. He wasn't out there like her brother, her father, and her late husband, fighting for truth, justice, and the American way. He just happened to be good at fighting fires. Not a nice job, not always safe. But necessary. Somebody had to do it, and he could, and he liked what he did.

Could Mary Jo accept that? Did she even want to try?

He fingered the twisted gold nugget that hung on a chain over Al Simpson's flag. She'd been good, he thought, studying her work. The piece was beautiful. A man would be proud to wear it and brag that his woman had created it for him.

She had loved her husband so much that

when he died she'd lost the ability to create beautiful jewelry. Did a woman get over a love that strong?

That Mary Jo might never be willing to let another man into her life was something Jack refused to contemplate. She was interested in him, attracted to him. He wasn't blind to that.

How far was she willing to go with him?

Before Jack realized what he was doing, he was at the top of the stairs, heading for her bedroom. She'd left the door open. He didn't go in. From the doorway he could see that she was still zonked.

He turned to go, but at the head of the stairs he spotted the door at the other end of the hall, the door her children weren't allowed to enter. The door that now stood open.

Jack couldn't resist and didn't try. In two seconds he was down the hall and through the door. What he saw there drew him to an immediate halt. Stunned, awed, he stared, trying to take it all in.

# SEVEN

Something woke her. The creak of a floorboard, the brush of denim on denim.

*Jack.*

Remembering the way he'd kissed her at the front door that morning, Mary Jo smiled before her eyes were open. She stretched like a cat lounging in the sun, feeling suddenly, sensuously, feminine.

Her clothes looked like they'd been slept in, which was only fair, since they had been. She didn't bother changing, but left her room in search of Jack.

She saw the back of him through the open door to her studio and knew a moment of embarrassment. The paintings were her private therapy, not meant for anyone's eyes. She hoped he didn't get the idea that she thought she was a real painter, as in an artist.

She entered the room and stood just behind him, but he seemed to not have noticed. "Jack?"

He turned slowly. "Mary Jo, these are so . . . powerful. They're . . . they're you, aren't they?"

Stunned, Mary Jo reared back. "No."

"Oh, yes," he said, looking at her, then the paintings. "Your other juices aren't the only ones that didn't dry up. These," he said, waving a hand at the canvases leaning against every inch of wall space around the room, "are . . . moving. I keep coming back to the word powerful."

"Jack." Flustered, Mary Jo smoothed her hair back with both hands. "They're not art, they're my therapy."

"Not art?" He gaped at her. "You're out of your mind."

"No, really. I use the canvas to work out my emotions so that someday I can work my way back to the creativity I lost."

"Not lost." Jack shook his head and turned back to the paintings. "Changed, maybe. You don't see it, do you?"

"There's . . . nothing to see."

Jack whirled on her, turning her by the shoulders until she faced the rest of the room. Standing behind her, he held her there. "Look at them," he urged. "Pretend you didn't do them yourself and *look*, Mary Jo. You have to see how good they are."

"No." Mary Jo shook her head. "I—"

Jack held her head still with his hands. "*Look.*"

As she stared at the stark splashes of grays and blacks, the swirls of purple, the angry dashes of red, Mary Jo felt the back of her neck start to tingle. "I . . ."

"It's your pain, your grief, Mary Jo, and it's . . . beautiful. I'm sorry. I'm not saying it right. Pain and grief aren't beautiful. But these paintings are."

Somehow, through Jack's words, Mary Jo began to see, really see what she'd been doing on her canvas. It wasn't just dreary, ugly colors. It wasn't just pain and grief. Her heart started pounding and her breath came faster and faster. It was . . . *art.*

"Jack," she breathed. "I . . ."

When she didn't go on, Jack studied the paintings spread out before him. If the darkest ones were the oldest . . . "Something changed," he said almost to himself. "These with the bright colors are newer. Something inside you changed. The red looks . . . angry. The yellow . . ."

"I see it," she cried. "I really see it!"

When she turned toward him, the glowing excitement in her eyes took Jack's breath away.

"Oh, Jack. The yellow is . . . well . . ." A light blush stole across her cheeks. She gripped his upper arms tightly. "It's . . . hope. Possibilities. It's you, Jack."

Jack sucked in his breath.

"It just . . . appeared there, the day we met. I didn't plan it, didn't even know I was doing it, but suddenly, that night of the car wreck, there it was, this big, cheerful blob of bright, sunny yellow."

Jack looped his arms around her waist and pulled her close, until their hips almost rested against each other. He couldn't help but grin. "So I'm a blob, am I?"

"No." As her eyes searched his face, so did her fingertips, sending tiny flames of heat to lick at Jack's nerves. "You're . . . possibilities," she whispered. "You're the future. You're here and now. Make love with me, Jack."

He'd felt it coming, knew—no, *hoped*—it was what she wanted. But he'd never had a woman come right out and ask him before, with words. Simple words. Words with more power to arouse than anything else she might have said or done.

"With pleasure," he whispered as he leaned to kiss her. Their lips met, and sparks tingled along Jack's nerves. He slipped his hands up her back and pulled her flush against him. Through her soft sweatshirt he felt the firmness of her woman's shape. His blood heated.

"Here," he whispered. "I want you right here, in this room."

"Yes." Her mouth, eager, insistent, took his. Took his mouth, took his breath, weakened his knees.

Oh, yes, he wanted her here, right here in this room where her emotions lived and breathed and covered the canvases. Where her past, her present, and her future came together in colors dark and light, swirling, bold colors that told him more about the woman she was than any words she'd ever spoken.

Scooping his hands underneath the hem of her sweatshirt, he touched smooth, velvet flesh, warm. Soft. He craved more, took more, running his palms up her ribs to just below her breasts.

When he stopped there, Mary Jo murmured a protest. She wanted his hands on her, everywhere. They were so warm, so hard yet gentle. Where he touched, she burned, and she wanted to go up in flames.

But Jack wouldn't be hurried. He wasn't after a quick blaze. He wanted to feel the embers smolder, let the heat build and build until it engulfed them both. He wanted her as needy as he was. The fine tremor in her hands on his face told him she was getting close. The thought of those delicate, graceful hands on other parts of his body threatened to test his control to the limits.

*Slowly*, he reminded himself. *Slowly*.

Mary Jo felt the heat building, felt Jack's deliberate slowness, and reveled in it. But fair was fair, she thought, and pulled the tail of his flannel shirt free of his jeans. When she at last touched his skin, she was gratified by the way his flesh rippled beneath her fingers.

"You like that," she murmured.

"I love that," he answered fervently. She was stirring the embers, sending sparks clear to the soles of his feet with her light touch on his back. "And this." He slid his hands up, pulling her sweatshirt up and off, letting it drop to the floor.

She might be sweatshirts and denim on the outside, or no-nonsense business suits like the one she'd had on the night of the fire, but underneath she was silk and satin. Silky skin, warm and pliant to the touch, satiny underwear, cool and slick. The contrast excited him.

His touch excited her. She returned the favor and pushed his shirt off. Oh, his chest was glorious. Broad and firmly muscled, with a light dusting of wiry hair that tickled her fingers. She touched, she tasted.

Fire shot straight to Jack's loins and set his pulse pounding rapidly. But no, he wouldn't hurry as his blood urged him to do.

*Slowly. Slowly.* He wanted, needed, to savor every moment, every inch of flesh, every sigh that breathed from her lips to his and back again. But he wanted to see her, too. All of her.

He leaned back in her arms and traced his fingers down the white satin straps of her bra, down the inner curve to the front clasp. "I want to take this off."

Her eyes glowed. Her lips curved upward at the corners. "Do you want help?"

The way his hands trembled, he might need it, but he shook his head and flipped the catch.

Mary Jo felt her breasts swell in anticipation of his touch. She closed her eyes and held her breath, waiting, needy, greedy to have his hands cover her. But they didn't. With the tip of one finger he pulled back first one cup, then the other, tormenting her with delicious anticipation. Then still with that one fingertip, he slid each strap in turn off her shoulder. The satin bra gleamed against the softer cotton of her sweatshirt on the floor.

The torment of his light touch as he trailed his fingers over her breasts made her groan. "Touch me, Jack. Touch me."

"I will," he promised. "But first I want to look my fill."

Mary Jo opened her eyes and saw him looking at her, at the contrast between his dark hand and her pale breast.

"So beautiful. Such delicate skin, I can see your veins."

"Feel," Mary Jo begged. She took his hands in hers and pressed his palms to her breasts, letting her eyes slide shut, showing him her need. "Yes."

"Yes." He made a growling sound deep in his throat and flexed his fingers around her, shaping her, holding her, driving her crazy.

Her own hands returned to his chest and caressed him. She not only needed his touch, she needed to touch him as well. So warm, so solid. Those wide shoulders, his strong neck, rippling back. "I love your body."

"You stole my line. But there's more." Trailing his fingers down her abdomen and causing her to suck in a sharp breath, he reached for the tab of her zipper and pulled it down slowly, so slowly that her hips twisted in protest.

Jack smiled. By the time he slid her jeans off to reveal another swath of white satin, this one across her hips, his game was backfiring on him. He'd wanted to drive her out of her mind, but it was himself he was tormenting. Yet he never wanted the torment to end.

Then she reached for his zipper to return the favor. He'd been hard from the first moment she'd touched him. Now, with her hand at his fly, he groaned with it. If she freed him now he would lose control. He pulled from her reach and slipped to his knees before her, kissing his way down her belly.

Her response, that sharp intake of breath, the subtle rippling of muscles beneath his mouth, went to his head like strong whiskey. He pulled her to the carpet with him.

They knelt facing each other, touching, tasting, feasting with eyes and lips and hands until it wasn't enough. Jack rolled to his back and took her with him until she was draped across his chest. This time she got his zipper down before he could think why he wanted to stop her. When she took him in her cool, soft hand his heart stopped and his hips rose sharply to meet her. One of the last few threads on his control snapped. Her smile was pure woman. She knew exactly what she was doing to him.

With a low growl, Jack kicked the rest of his clothes off, then peeled hers away. Rolling until she lay on her back with him cradled between her thighs, he settled his mouth over the taut tip of one breast. Her gasp, the way she arched up to meet him, snapped another thread on his control.

Her hands were all over him, touching, grasping. His returned the favor. Breath, harsh and scarce, mingled. Hearts thundered, pulses raced. Thought melted away as pure sensation took over. With a hand between her legs he found her ready, made her whimper in need.

Another roll and she was on top of him, straddling him, taking him into her body, all of him, to the hilt.

Mary Jo threw back her head and savored the fullness of having him inside her. His hands went to her hips to guide the motion he needed, and it was what she needed too. She went wild, riding him there on the floor in the room where her emotions flowed from canvas to canvas, and now, to Jack.

The pleasure inside her erupted suddenly, violently. She cried out Jack's name. Instantly he followed her over the edge.

When his mind cleared enough for rational thought, Jack fought off a shudder. He didn't want to acknowledge that making love with Mary Jo had changed him, but it was hard to ignore. Something inside him had . . . shifted. A part of her was now a part of him, and he was a part of her. He wondered if she felt it as strongly as he did, but decided to keep it to himself for now.

Without a word, he shifted her, lifted her into his arms, and carried her to her bed.

Her eyes opened slowly with a smile. "More?"

Jack met her gaze, hoping he didn't look as bewildered as he felt. "If you're willing. I may never get enough of you."

Her eyes turned dark and she held him tighter. "I know."

They made love twice more, then Jack retrieved his pager from his jeans in the other room. He turned the setting from vibrate to tone and put it on the night stand, then curled up with Mary Jo. They slept in each other's arms.

At dawn Sunday morning Mary Jo was in that state of half-sleep, where the mind worked slowly, but the body refused to work at all. Her mind drifted dreamily through the night past and relived that moment when she first realized she was going to make love with Jack.

She dozed again, smiling, and roused to feel Jack's hand on her bare hip. Willing herself back to sleep, she let her mind drift again until it hit on something that sent her sitting bolt upright in bed, wide awake, heart pounding in sudden fear.

"He was here!"

Jack was only a second behind her. "Who?" he demanded, picking up instantly on her tension.

"The caller. He was in the house."

Jack was out of bed in less than a second. "Just now? Did you hear him?"

"No." Mary Jo grabbed his hand to keep him from rushing out of the room stark naked to confront an intruder long gone. "No. I'm sorry. It was the other day. I just remembered—"

"You just now remembered that the man who's threatening you was in your house?" he asked, his voice rising.

"I just realized it. I came home to find the back door open. I blamed Andy."

"When?"

"It was . . . the Monday after the fire."

"Which fire?"

"Oh my word, maybe *both* of them," she admitted, remembering. "The Sunday after the first fire, we came home from church and I found the back door unlocked. Andy was outside, and I didn't say anything to him. It's his job to make sure the back door is locked. Then you came over, to check our smoke alarms," she added with a mock glare.

"Hey, it's a living."

"It was an excuse, and a pitiful one, at that."

"It got me some of your mama's fried chicken. Are you sure Andy didn't just forget to check the door before you left for church?"

Mary Jo sighed and shook her head. "No, I'm not sure. He *said* he checked it. But that second time, yes. It was the day you were out on the ladder banging on the house. I made sure the door was locked myself before I went out and got the kids. We went to Mother's for supper. When we came back, you were gone, and the . . . Jack, you didn't—"

"Break into your house? Hell no."

"I remember feeling . . . creepy that night, thinking someone had been in the house."

"Why didn't you call the police?"

"And tell them what? That I thought the back door was locked, but maybe it wasn't?" She shook her head again.

"You think it was the caller."

"It makes sense, if he really thinks I have the watches."

Jack frowned. "Yeah. You could be right. I don't like it. I think you should talk to Dalton."

"He said if I talked to the police he would

know, and something would happen to Andy or Heather. I can't take that chance, Jack."

Jack sat on the edge of the bed and threaded his fingers through hers. "The kids aren't here, Mary Jo. Call your mother and tell her to stay away for a couple more days. Give Dalton a chance."

"And you didn't call me?" Dalton demanded. "What the hell were you thinking?"

"I wasn't thinking," Mary Jo confessed as Dalton stared her down in her living room Sunday afternoon. "I was reacting. I got Andy and Heather away from here where no one can find them. It wasn't until later—this morning, actually—that I remembered about the back door."

"Nobody can find them," Dalton muttered. "Hell, I could find them blindfolded. Your mother took them to their other grandparents in Oklahoma. Don't look so shocked. I'm not psychic, just logical."

"Do you think he'll find them?" Fear tightened her throat. "I called this morning to tell them to stay there until they heard back from me. I guess they were at church. I left a message on the answering machine. He won't find them, will he?" she asked again.

"I don't think he'll go to the trouble. Tell me again everything he said."

Mary Jo repeated everything she remembered.

"You're sure you didn't recognize the voice?"

She shook her head. "He sounded muffled, like maybe he was speaking through a handkerchief or something."

"But you're positive it was a man."

"Yes."

Jack slipped his fingers through Mary Jo's and squeezed her hand for support. Mary Jo didn't even think to feel self-conscious that Dalton was watching.

"Did you hear the voice?" Dalton asked Jack.

"No."

Dalton took a deep breath, then let it out. "Okay, what we've got then are two separate crimes, two separate perps."

"That's how we figured it," Jack said.

Dalton raised an eyebrow and glanced again at their joined hands. One corner of his mouth twitched upward. "We?"

Jack waited until Dalton met his gaze. "That's right. We."

Dalton paused, then nodded. "Okay. Mary Jo, you left the store that night right at five, you said."

"Yes."

"By the time you filled up your mother's gas tank, dropped clothes off at the dry cleaners, went to the grocery store, then back to the store, it was about five-thirty."

"That fits with the time the fire was called in," Jack said. "Thompson, over at the hotel across the square, called in and reported seeing smoke in the jewelry store at five thirty-three."

Dalton sat on the wingback chair. "No one was seen entering or leaving the store except Mary Jo when she left at five, and when she came back at five-thirty. So between five and five-thirty somebody jiggles the lock on the back door, comes in and takes the watches from the safe, goes back out the same way he came in. The second perp must have also gone in the back. He comes in to steal the watches, planning to set a fire in hopes that everyone will think the watches were destroyed in the blaze."

"Only the watches aren't there," Mary Jo said.

"So he panics, then gets mad that somebody beat him there, and sets the fire anyway."

"And he figures the only person who could have taken the watches was Mary Jo."

"Why would he think that?" Mary Jo asked.

"Because there is no one else," Jack said.

"But how would some stranger know that?"

Jack and Dalton shared a look.

"What aren't you telling me?" she demanded.

Jack looked at Dalton. "Are you thinking what I'm thinking?"

Dalton's expression went blank. "No proof.

Mary Jo, tell me again everyone who knew about the watches."

Mary Jo gave Dalton and Jack a narrow-eyed glare for excluding her from their little byplay, but that was all right. She had her own suspicions, and they weren't pretty. "Me," she answered to Dalton. "Bob, of course. The UPS man who delivered them. No telling how many people at the wholesaler's who shipped the watches. The customer who was there when they arrived. And I'm sure Bob told the customer who ordered them that we were expecting the shipment and when it was due."

Dalton checked the notes he'd made when he and Jack had questioned her the morning after the fire. "Of those people, who knew the safe was broken?"

"Bob and I. Then there are the people in Amarillo who were supposed to have already fixed it. They wouldn't know exactly what was in the safe, but they would surely assume that there would be jewelry there."

"What about a cleaning crew?"

"No." Mary Jo shook her head. "Karen, Bob's wife, does what cleaning Bob and I don't do ourselves."

"Have you had an electrician in there since the safe's been broken? A repairman? Any other people been in Bob's office to know about the safe?"

"Maybe," Mary Jo said with a shrug. "You know I only work three days a week. But there's no one else I can specifically name."

"And of all those people," Jack said to Dalton, "who is the most likely person to think he'd know what was going on at the police station well enough to know if Mary Jo called the cops on her caller?"

"Well, that narrows it down, doesn't it?" Mary Jo frowned. "At least I'm not the only one to come up with Bob's name."

"No," Jack said with a laugh. "You're just the last."

"Get real. You thought it was me."

"It's hard to figure," Dalton said, half to himself. "He's the county sheriff's cousin. He doesn't have an extravagant lifestyle, at least not so that anyone would notice. He doesn't have kids, and his wife works. What could he need money for so badly that he would rob and torch his own store?"

"Maybe it isn't him," Mary Jo said hopefully. "Maybe there's something we've overlooked."

"Yeah." Dalton stood and tucked his notebook back into his pocket. "Like who beat him to the watches. I'll see what I can find out without letting anyone know I've talked to you. You've taken care of the phone, so if your caller calls back we'll know where he calls from, and we'll have his voice on tape."

On his way to the door Dalton allowed that perhaps he'd overlooked something when checking out the UPS man and the safe company.

"Don't forget the customer," Mary Jo reminded him. Her eyes widened. "I just remembered. Neither Bob nor I knew he was there Friday afternoon until we walked out to the showroom as Bob was leaving. Maybe he overheard us complaining to each other about the safe."

Dalton patted the notebook in his pocket. "I've got his name here. I'll check him out again."

"Dalton." Mary Jo stopped him as he was leaving. "I'm supposed to go to work tomorrow."

He nodded. "Fine. Just go and do your job. No poking around, no asking questions, you hear? We don't know it's Bob, but we don't know it isn't."

"Don't worry," Jack said. "I'll stop by a time or two and check on her."

Dalton's lips quirked. "From the looks of things, you're sure taking your assignment, ah, personally, shall we say."

Mary Jo frowned at both men. "What assignment?"

Dalton got a funny look on his face, as though he'd just accidentally swallowed a goldfish. "I'm outta here." Dalton opened the door and stepped out. "I'll check with both of you tomorrow."

Mary Jo closed the door after Dalton and turned on Jack. "What assignment? What was he grinning about?"

"Uh . . . no comment."

# EIGHT

*"What?"*

"Well, hell, Mary Jo, you don't expect me to repeat it, do you?"

"No thank you." If looks could kill, Jack would have been a dead man the instant he confessed that he had agreed to Dalton's request that he stick close to Mary Jo and keep an eye on her.

"It sounded bad enough the first time," Mary Jo went on. "Dalton was right. You take your responsibilities too seriously. But somehow I doubt he expected you to stick as close to me as you got last night."

Jack closed his eyes. "Why did I know you were going to say that?"

"What else am I supposed to think? Up until yesterday you were still half convinced I was the arsonist and thief."

"I was not."

"Could have fooled me."

"A blind man could have fooled you. You see only what you want to see." Jack ran a hand over his face in frustration. "Dammit, you can't think last night had anything to do with Dalton or arson."

Sickness churned in Mary Jo's stomach. Had she been a lonely, gullible fool last night? Was Jack silently laughing at how easy she'd been? They barely knew each other, yet she'd tumbled into his arms and invited him into her bed.

"Don't."

Mary Jo glared at him, "Don't what?"

"Don't start finding ulterior motives for what happened between us last night."

"Then suppose you tell me what did happen."

*I fell in love*, Jack thought, the shock of it settling around him like a blanket. But he couldn't tell her that. She was in no mood to believe him. In truth, it was going to take some getting used to from his side of the equation, too.

"Last night," he said softly, "was quite simply the most incredible night of my life."

Tears stung the back of Mary Jo's throat. Oh, God, she wanted to believe him, because his words described what last night had been for her, too.

"It happened," he added, "because I couldn't stay away from you. You were in my mind day and night from the minute we met. If you can't trust me after what we shared last night—"

His pager was beeping. "Dammit." He checked the message and swore. "Grass fire." He looked back at her, his expression grim. "This conversation isn't over, and neither are we. I'll be back as soon as I can."

Mary Jo was shaking her head as he turned to go. "No, Jack. I think I need some time to myself, time to think."

"Then you think fast, darlin', because I'm coming back the first chance I get."

"Fool." Mary Jo made a face at herself in the mirror. "Either you trust him or you don't. Make up your mind."

In fact, there seemed to be no decision to make. She had decided to trust Jack with all of her, body and soul, the night before. For her, there was no turning back.

She didn't really believe he'd had ulterior motives for making love with her. That was just her insecurities rearing their pointy little heads, trying to get her to tuck herself back into her shell of isolation where life was safe.

And lonely. Well, to hell with her insecurities. She very much liked it out in the world, particularly when that world included one Jack Riley. As soon as he came back, she would tell him so.

Right after she made him squirm for agreeing to spy on her. The jerk.

But the wind picked up, the grass fire spread, and Jack didn't make it back. Not that afternoon, nor that evening, nor that night. His volunteer crew had swelled with the influx of area farmers and ranchers who came to help battle the blaze before it jumped the creek and took out Harley Fenster's pasture that was bone dry, just like everything else in the county.

It was a bitch, made worse by Jack seeing Mary Jo's hurt, accusing eyes in every billow of smoke. Dammit, she couldn't possibly think . . . whatever it was she was thinking. She had to know he had feelings for her, deep feelings.

And if he didn't keep his mind on his work there wouldn't be anything left of him to send back to her but ashes.

Mary Jo didn't sleep worth a damn. When she wasn't worrying about Jack and the grass fire, she was worrying about facing Bob Yates the next morning and acting like she didn't suspect him of being the creep who'd called her and threatened her children.

Really, she thought he was the least likely person to do something dishonest. He was always so nice and pleasant, easy to work with. The only reason she'd come up with his name at all as a possible suspect was the same reason Dalton and Jack had at first wondered about her—there simply was no one else.

Yet she had been innocent. Maybe Bob was, too. Maybe all of them were overlooking something obvious. Maybe there was some detail she'd forgotten to tell Dalton. He was good at his job, according to everyone in town. A former Texas Ranger, he had the respect and admiration of the entire community. But if there was something she'd forgotten to tell him, something important, even he could arrive at an erroneous conclusion.

And all of this speculation was getting Mary Jo nowhere. She had wool-gathered so long she was going to be late to work if she didn't hurry. She would just breeze into the store as if nothing were wrong, as if Bob's name as a possible suspect had never crossed her mind.

Besides, it was crazy to think it was him. Sure, he could collect insurance for the damages and theft, but he would have to sink that money right back into the store for repairs and new merchandise. He had nothing to gain.

Mary Jo felt much better after drawing that conclusion and was able to go into the store and greet Bob as usual.

"Well, what do you think?" Bob smiled and

held out his arms to draw her attention to the room at large.

Mary Jo noted the fresh paint, the new carpet, the spotless glass of the display case. "As good as new. I like the new plant." The old ficus tree that had been in the front window would definitely not be missed. The absurd thought crossed her mind that maybe, if Bob were the culprit, he hadn't been after insurance money. Maybe he'd just wanted that ugly plant replaced.

*You're losing it, Mary Jo.*

Although, come to think of it, had the idea crossed her mind she might have been tempted herself to set fire to the store if a new plant were in the deal.

"Wait until you see our new offices," Bob said eagerly.

Mary Jo followed him behind the counter and down the hall to his office, where the fire had started. She hadn't seen the room after the fire but she assumed it had been gutted. Now it was very nice indeed, with new paint and carpet, all new furniture and file cabinets, and even a new plant hanging in front of the window to the alley.

"Isn't it beautiful?" Bob asked. "I'm going to enjoy working in nice surroundings for a change."

Mary Jo chuckled. "If all you were after was a little redecorating, we could have done that without the fire."

The instant the words left her mouth she wanted them back.

"Yeah, well." Bob's laugh had an odd ring to it, as if forced. "This way the insurance paid for it."

"Uh, right. What about my office?" Without waiting for him she spun out of the room and went to the end of the hall, to the cubbyhole where she'd kept track of the paperwork and Karen ran the monthly financial reports and balanced the bank statements. Here, too, the room had been refurbished. There was even another plant, complete with its own plant light, since there was no window. A dainty little African violet in full bloom. She loved African violets.

"Do you like it?" Bob's voice now held the note of a young boy anxious to please.

Mary Jo felt like a jerk. "Of course I do. How pretty. Thank you." She turned toward him and smiled. "It was nice of you to get it. I really appreciate it." *Shut up before you overdo it, Mary Jo.*

She put her purse in the bottom drawer of the new desk and hung her coat in the tiny closet between her office and Bob's. "Have we had any customers this morning?"

"No." Bob ducked his head. "I have more bad news though. We don't have phone service yet."

"Why on earth not, after all this time?"

"There was a problem with the wiring. It was all burned and melted. They've been replacing it. They worked all weekend. If we're lucky we'll be all hooked up by this afternoon."

"I hope so. Without phone service we can't take credit cards."

"I know," he said grimly. "But there's more, Mary Jo."

"More bad news?"

Bob nodded. "The Rolexes in the safe weren't the only things stolen."

Alarm bells went off inside Mary Jo's head. "They weren't?"

Bob shook his head and led her out to the display case. "I didn't realize it until yesterday, but look." He pointed at the long case that was the center of the display.

Mary Jo stared at the jewelry and immediately noticed something was wrong. "Things have been moved. Where's the pear-shaped pendant?"

"And the emerald cut garnet, and the ruby teardrop earrings."

Mary Jo closed her eyes. This was not possible. She distinctly remembered looking at the display case when she came back to the store that Friday night. She *always* glanced at the case when she came through the door.

*Think. Think.*

Hadn't the missing items been there that night? *Hadn't they?*

The front door opened; the bell overhead jingled.

Mary Jo looked up from the display case too stunned by this latest development to school her expression when Jack walked in. By the time she realized it was him, she was so relieved to see him unhurt that she drank him in with her eyes.

"Good morning," he said quietly. Expectantly.

Shaken by how glad she was to see him in one piece, Mary Jo looked away. She thought she'd made up her mind last night to trust him, but now doubts assailed her.

"Hey, Jack." Bob greeted him as though nothing were wrong, when, as far as Mary Jo was concerned, everything was wrong. "Since you're here, does this mean that grass fire is out?"

"It's out." Jack gave a single nod to Bob, but his eyes were on Mary Jo.

"Praise the Lord," Bob said fervently. "So then, what can we do for you this morning?"

"I was hoping you weren't busy so I could have a word with Mary Jo."

Bob sobered. "More questions about the fire. Certainly. I understand. I was just showing her where some additional items are missing that we hadn't noticed before."

Lines formed across Jack's brow. "No fooling? Something besides the Rolexes is missing?"

"Yes," Bob said gravely.

"Have you told Dalton?" Jack asked.

"No, actually. I just discovered it last night when I was seeing to some last-minute details before reopening. I told Harry. He was here when I discovered it. He said he'd tell Dalton. I was just getting ready to call the insurance company and update our claim. If the inventory disk and printouts hadn't been destroyed in the fire we could have checked everything off and discovered what was missing a week ago."

Something clicked in the back of Mary Jo's mind. "Oh, my word, I just remembered."

"Remembered what?" both men demanded.

"The night of the fire. When I came back and grabbed Andy's backpack I thought I might as well work on the year-end inventory at home. I'd promised you I would get it straightened out while you were gone. I picked up the disk and printouts to take with me. I can't believe I forgot about them all this time."

"So you have them at home?" Bob asked cautiously.

"I . . . damn, what did I do with them? I know I picked them up, but I don't remember . . ." She shook her head in frustration. Closing her eyes, she concentrated on that night, on her movements in the cubbyhole before she discovered the fire.

"It would help if we had them," Bob said, "but if you don't remember . . . well, we have to assume the information was destroyed in the fire."

"No," Mary Jo said slowly, aware that Jack was watching her like a hawk. "I put the disk . . . in my pocket, and the paperwork . . . I can't remember if I put it in my purse or in Andy's backpack. But I'm sure it's at home, Bob. I'll run over there right now—except," she added, frustrated again. "Come to think of it, I don't remember seeing that purse since then. Or the clothes I had on, for that matter. I've got it! Mother took everything to the cleaners to get the smoke smell out. The disk and printouts were in my suit pocket. Let me grab my purse and I'll go down there right now and—"

"Oh, no. Don't bother," Bob said quickly. "That wind will cut through you like a knife. Isn't that right, Jack?"

Jack pursed his lips and nodded. "It's a sharp one, all right."

"Just bring the disk or whatever you find in tomorrow," Bob said. "That will be plenty soon enough. What a relief. I had a hard enough time getting the insurance company to pay up on the Rolexes without paperwork to back up my claim. They finally backtracked the shipment to the wholesaler to verify it. I couldn't begin to tell them where all this other jewelry came from without our records."

"And still," Jack offered, "they'd only have your word that you hadn't sold it before the fire."

Bob's eyes widened. "You're right." Staring thoughtfully at the floor for a moment, he finally nodded. "I'll call them this morning and tell them what's going on, and that we should have at least some of our paperwork in-house by to-morrow. That should do it."

Still muttering to himself, Bob left the show-room and went back to his office.

Mary Jo's heart was pounding. Things were very fishy, to her way of thinking. "Where's Dal-ton?" she whispered to Jack.

"He got called down to Austin first thing this morning to testify for the prosecution in a car-jacking case." He pulled a notepad from his pocket and scribbled while he spoke. "I'm sorry I didn't make it back last night."

Mary Jo didn't want to think about last night and how angry she'd been, but neither could she tell Jack what was on her mind with Bob in the next room. "I hear the fire was a bad one."

"Bad enough."

"Was anybody hurt?"

"No." He handed her the notepad. It read: I thought you said nothing else was missing after the fire?

I DID, she wrote in big letters. I KNOW THE GARNET WAS HERE. NOW IT'S NOT.

"Are you still mad at me?" Jack asked quietly.

Mary Jo looked into his eyes and couldn't read them. He looked the way she imagined she would if she were trying to keep someone from knowing she was hurt.

The thought was a revelation. Had she hurt

him yesterday by accusing him of sleeping with her just to further the investigation? She shook her head. "I don't know. I need to think about it."

"Don't."

"Don't what?"

"Don't think about it. Just tell me how you feel."

"Confused. Uncertain."

He gave her a wry smile. "Welcome to the club. I'm tied up with paperwork today, clear through lunch, but I'd like to see you tonight."

Mary Jo tilted her head. "Getting humble, Jack?"

"Why do you ask?"

"You've never asked to see me. You've always just shown up whenever it suited you."

"If I'd asked, you might have said no. I wasn't willing to take that chance."

"Now you are?"

"Forget it. The only thing you really have a choice about is if I come over before supper or after. Either way, I'm coming over."

She gave him a wry smile. "That's my Jack."

"Am I? Am I yours?"

"Do you want to be?"

"In a heartbeat, darlin'. From my head to my toes."

A shiver of what could only be called antici-pation raced down Mary Jo's spine. The man knew how to get to her, that was for sure.

He was scribbling on his notepad again. When he finished he turned it toward her. It read: Just act natural and wait for Dalton. The situation stinks. Keep your eyes and ears open. I love you.

Mary Jo read that last sentence again, then, her heart in her throat, jerked her head up to stare dumbfounded at Jack.

He grinned and shrugged, holding his hands out palms up. "It's true." Before she could think what to say, he was gone.

Mary Jo was as jumpy as a cat all day. She spilled coffee on the display case—thank heaven none of it landed on the new carpet—broke a fingernail, and counted out the wrong change to a customer twice before getting it right. She was torn between staring at Bob and trying to read his guilt or innocence on his face and in his actions, and not looking at him at all for fear he might read her thoughts and know she thought him a thief. Maybe an arsonist, too.

Then there was Jack, who never left her thoughts.

*I love you.* Casually scrawled at the bottom of his note. She might have been able to laugh it off, despite that it hurt to think he would joke about something so serious. If only she hadn't looked at him. If only he hadn't told her it was true.

Maybe he didn't mean that. Maybe he meant it was true that the situation stank.

And maybe between Jack, the fire, the theft, her boss, and Dalton not showing up when she kept expecting to see him any minute all afternoon, she was going to lose her mind.

She missed her children desperately, and missed being able to call her mother.

For that matter, she missed being able to call anyone. Damn the phone company. It was after four before the phones were finally working.

Business was so light during most of the day that Mary Jo had time to go through the boxes of smoke- and water-stained paperwork that had survived the fire. She searched diligently, without letting on to Bob, for the inventory papers, but didn't find them. She was once again positive that she'd picked them up the night of the fire. She just couldn't remember what she'd done with them.

At half past four Bob came to the door of her cubbyhole office. "Why don't you knock off early? That way you can run by the dry cleaners before they close at five and see if they have that paperwork."

"Good idea. Thanks."

"How are your kids, by the way? I haven't heard you mention them today."

Ice formed in Mary Jo's veins. Bob *never* asked about her kids. Why now? Why right after the mention of the missing paperwork? She forced a smile. "They're fine." She grabbed her purse from the bottom desk drawer. "I think I'll take you up on your offer and leave early."

"Fine." Bob nodded. "Good. That's . . . good." He followed as she got her coat, slipped it on, and headed for the front door. "Oh, Mary Jo," he called as she was leaving. "If you find that paperwork, why don't you give me a call? That way I can put it out of my mind."

Mary Jo answered with a nod and a wave and went out the door. If she moved a little faster than normal—okay, so she practically ran— maybe no one noticed.

But someone did notice. She was watched until her car disappeared around the corner and was out of sight of the square.

# NINE

"These are the items he says are missing." Mary Jo pointed to the items on the list. The inventory diskette and printout had been in the pocket of her suit. Her mother hadn't checked before taking it to the cleaners; she'd just wanted the smelly garments out of the house. The cleaners had saved the items for her.

Mary Jo had called Bob and told him she had the items. Jack and Dalton had been beside her when she'd placed the call.

"How sure are you that they were there the night of the fire?"

"Come on, Dalton." Jack shot him a hard look. "She's answered that question three times already this evening."

"And I'll answer it again," Mary Jo said sharply. "I'm positive about the garnet. The security light was shining right on it. I'm not positive about the rest, but I think if anything was missing I would have noticed when I walked past the counter."

"Why do you think you'd notice?" Dalton asked again.

"Because I stare at that counter for hours at a time when business is slow. I know every piece that's there, and I know where each one belongs. I'm the one who usually arranges the merchandise in the case. I would know if things were moved or missing. Now let me ask you a question," she said to Dalton. "Did Harry Yates tell you about any of this?"

"Not a word."

"Bob says Harry was with him last night when he realized things were missing, and that Harry was supposed to tell you about it."

Dalton shook his head. "He didn't call me at home last night and I was in the office maybe five minutes, at six this morning, before I left for Austin."

"You don't think Harry's in on it, too, do you?" she asked.

"We don't know that either of them are in on it, Mary Jo. Even if the watches were the only things missing the night of the fire, anybody could have taken that other jewelry afterward. Workmen were all over that place for days. Hell, for that matter, firemen were all over the place that night after the fire."

"You accusing my men?" Jack's voice was quiet steel.

"I'm not accusing anyone," Dalton said calmly. "Not even Bob. We still don't have any real evidence. I can't charge somebody just because my gut tells me to."

"The showcase is kept locked," Mary Jo reminded them. "As far as I know, the locks weren't broken. Unless Bob had them replaced and just didn't tell me. Oh, never mind," she added. "There's a spare set of keys in Bob's desk."

"Great security he's got," Dalton said with disgust.

"What do we do now?" Mary Jo asked.

"You do nothing," Dalton said. "You let me do my job."

"But how am I supposed to do my job? He expectes me to come to work in the morning and bring the disk and paperwork with me. How am I supposed to face him again, spend another entire day with him, when there's every possibility he robbed his own store and set the fire that almost killed me?"

Jack reached out and placed a hand on her shoulder. "You don't need to go in. Call in sick."

Mary Jo threw her hands in the air. "That will solve everything."

In a house on the other side of town, a phone rang. It was answered quickly, quietly, before anyone else could pick it up.

"Your time's up," the voice on the other end said.

It was the syndicate. The one he owed thousands—tens of thousands—of dollars to. "No!" Sweat beaded across his upper lip and along his spine. His mouth went dry. "Another day. That's all I need, another day."

"You said that last week, pal. And do you remember what I said?"

Bile rose in his throat. He wasn't likely to forget the promise of broken bones if he didn't pay on time. "I just ran into a little problem, that's all. I just need a little more time. Just a little more."

A heavy sigh came over the phone. "Noon tomorrow. That's it, pal. And the interest has gone up."

"Wh-what do you mean?"

"This extra time costs us money. So it costs you. You pay us what you owe us by noon tomorrow, or they won't ever find all the pieces of you. You'll be scattered in little bitty chunks from here to the Rio Grande."

The phone when dead.

Oh God, oh God, what was he going to do?

Okay. Okay. Stay calm. He had to stay calm.

"Who was that on the phone?" came a soft voice from the kitchen.

"No one," he called back. "Wrong number."

Oh God. They were going to kill him. He *had* to get those watches back.

Mary Jo's phone rang. The Caller ID box read "Out of Area." "Maybe it's Mother," Mary Jo said hopefully.

It wasn't. Jack knew by the way the blood drained from her face. He swore sharply. "It's him," he muttered to Dalton as he reached over and pushed the record button on the answering machine. "Probably calling from a cell phone."

"Yes," Mary Jo finally said, her voice shaking. "I know the place. Yes. Midnight? But— A-All right." Slowly she hung up the phone and reached for Jack's hand.

The trap was laid. If everything went according to plan, the man threatening Mary Jo would be caught and in custody by twelve-thirty that night.

He'd told Mary Jo to take the watches to the abandoned barn twelve miles east of town at midnight. She was to drive there alone and park behind the structure. If he didn't show up by twelve-thirty she was to leave the watches under the overturned barrel that would be next to the old corral gate.

Dalton had the disk and inventory sheets,

should they become necessary as evidence later. He would be watching the old barn from some nearby concealment, although where he thought he could hide his car in that part of the county was beyond Mary Jo. If she had trouble or got scared she was to use the handheld two-way radio unit he'd given her and he and two deputies would come running.

But it was Jack Mary Jo was worried about. The grim set to his jaw and the way he kept muttering, "Ten minutes. Just give me ten minutes alone with the bastard," had both Mary Jo and Dalton a little concerned.

"Look," Mary Jo finally told him. "I'm scared enough about this as it is."

"I know you are, darlin'." He wrapped his arms around her and pulled her to his chest, rubbing his hands up and down her back. "I promise, I won't let anything happen to you."

"That," she said, pushing away from him, "is one of the things I'm scared of. I'm going to expend half of my nerves worrying about what you're going to do." His job was to hide in the backseat of her car. He'd nearly fought Dalton for the privilege. Dalton had only conceded when Jack threatened to follow Mary Jo and blow the whole setup.

"Is there something the two of you would like to tell me?" Dalton asked.

"You stay out of this," Jack said with a snarl.

"Your mouth has already gotten me in enough trouble."

"Me?" Dalton protested. "What have I done?"

"Nothing," Mary Jo assured him. "Except reveal a truth I wasn't supposed to know about."

Dalton looked at Mary Jo's lowered brow, Jack's bunched jaw. "Oops."


Mary Jo's nerves stretched just past the point of tautness. "Are you warm enough back there?"

From his cramped spot on the floorboard of the backseat, Jack grimaced. "I'll survive. But only if you slow down. How fast are you going? We want to get there alive."

"Put a sock in it, Jack."

"Guess that answers my earlier question," he muttered.

"What question?"

"About whether or not you're still mad at me."

"Should I be?"

"No. You shouldn't. I meant what I said at the end of my note."

*I love you* had been at the end of his note. Mary Jo's hands tightened on the steering wheel. "Now's a fine time to tell me."

"Is that all you have to say? A man tells you he loves you, and you complain about his timing?"

"Hang on," she warned as she braked for the turn onto the short stretch of rutted dirt road that led to the abandoned barn. "We're here."

Jack's response was a series of muffled oaths as he was bounced up and down and thrown head-first against the back door.

"Sorry," Mary Jo muttered.

When she hit a deep pothole he let out a particularly loud curse.

"Would you keep it down back there? They can probably hear you in the next county."

"Dammit, Mary Jo." He rose up on his knees, in fear of having his head bashed in at the next pothole.

Mary Jo put a hand on his head and shoved. "Would you stay *down*? If he's here he'll see you. You're making me a nervous wreck."

Mary Jo parked behind the abandoned barn and waited.

Police Chief Dalton McShane, Office Charlie McCommis, and Officer Gary Wilhelm, each in his own unit, found his own nearby place to wait and watch.

The man they all waited for was busy breaking in—for the third time, he thought with fury—through the back door of Mary Jo's house. This time he knew the watches weren't here. She had them with her, waiting for him to show up at the old barn.

The fool. Did she actually think he was going to show himself to her?

But he was after more than the watches this time. Now he needed the inventory printouts and disk. They had to be destroyed so he could falsify the insurance claim to get enough money to get the goons off his back.

That's how he thought of the syndicate that had bankrolled that last bet of his. Goons.

Oh, he'd thought highly enough of them at first. Until the phone calls had started. The threats.

They were no better than crooks. Loan sharks. Blood suckers. Preying on a man with a weakness for gambling, dangling money under his nose, sucking him in with greasy smiles and false promises.

Christ. If Harry or the rest of the family ever found out what he was into they would collectively croak. Ol' law-and-order Harry, a chip off his old man's block. Cousin Harry never let Bob forget for a minute while they were growing up that Bob's daddy had gotten himself shot and killed trying to rob a gas station and that Harry's old man, the U.S. marshal, had taken Bob to raise as his own.

Assholes, the whole lot of them. He'd show them. He would get the watches. That would get one man off his back and get him the money to pay off the goons. This time tomorrow, Bob Yates would be sitting pretty.

Damn his hide, he should never have let Mary Jo and his wife take over the bookkeeping at the store. None of this would have been necessary if he'd been able to skim a little now and then. But between the two of them and their eagle eyes, that had been impossible.

So here he was, once again reduced to common criminal activities. He eased the back door shut and turned on his flashlight. No small, discreet penlight this time. He'd brought his heavy-duty flashlight, the one he kept in his trunk for highway emergencies. He was not leaving this house without the inventory data.

"We're here," Mary Jo said quietly into Dalton's radio unit. "No sign of anyone."

"We see you," came Dalton's response.

"Where are you?" she asked.

"Close. Don't use the radio unless you have to."

"Where?" she insisted. "There's no place to hide a car out here."

"I'm in the barn right beside you. Now stay off the radio."

"Well," Jack said from the backseat, "I guess that eliminates my first choice for how to pass the next half hour."

Mary Jo tensed. "Here comes a car."

Jack leaned forward to peer over her shoulder toward the highway that led from town.

Unconsciously Mary Jo gripped the hand he'd placed on the top of her seat back. "It's slowing down. Look."

The car did indeed slow down. It stopped just before it would have been hidden from their view by the barn that sat between them and the highway.

"Why's he stopping way out there?"

"It might not be him," Jack cautioned. "I can't make out the car, but it doesn't look familiar."

The driver got out walked in front of his headlights.

"Looks like Butch Peterson," Jack noted.

"He's going down into those tall weeds in the bar ditch." Mary Jo leaned forward and stared hard. "What's he doing?"

Jack started laughing.

"What's so funny? I can't tell . . . Oh, good grief." She could see plainly enough now that a car was coming from the east. The beam from its headlights was just broad enough to enable her to realize that Butch Peterson was standing in the weeds beside the road taking a leak. "That idiot."

"I'll say." Jack was still laughing. "It's colder than hell out there. He's liable to freeze something off."

"He's probably too drunk to notice," she grumbled.

❖————————❖

What Mary Jo failed to notice was the make of the car that had caught Butch Peterson in its headlights. Had she been paying attention, she might have realized that the car heading east toward town was her mother's.

The message Mary Jo had left on the Simpsons' answering machine Sunday, that Arliss should not bring the children home, had alarmed Arliss as well as the Simpsons. Arliss had at first decided to do just as Mary Jo asked. But by late Sunday night she'd been frantic with worry. Monday she had tried to call Mary Jo and had been unable to reach her at home or at work.

Arliss had had enough suspense. With the Simpsons agreeing to keep Andy and Heather a few more days, Arliss had gotten in her car Monday afternoon and driven straight for Two Oaks.

It had been the trip from hell. She'd left the Simpsons in such a rush that she'd forgotten her watch and her favorite earrings. On the way she'd lost a fan belt and precious time in western Oklahoma and had a flat miles away from any town just across the line into Texas. More time lost.

Now it was after midnight and she was going to scare Mary Jo to death bursting in on her this late, but it couldn't be helped. Mary Jo should not have left such a cryptic message on the answering machine. Arliss wanted to know what was going on, and she wanted to know immediately. She wouldn't even go home and call. She was going straight to her daughter's house.

When she pulled into Mary Jo's driveway at about 12:15 A.M. the house was dark. Arliss used her key to let herself in through the front door.

After searching the first floor, then upstairs in the bedrooms, and still not finding the damned disk and printout, Bob Yates was just coming downstairs when he heard someone at the front door.

*Damn the bitch. It's not 12:30 yet. What is she doing home?*

Panic shot through him. She was going to get him caught. In jail he might be safe from the buddy who'd gotten him mixed up in the watch deal, but he would never be out of reach of the goons he owed money to. He couldn't get caught. Couldn't afford to.

When the woman came through the front door, he was ready. He raised his flashlight, and with all his might, swung it down on her head. The impact made a sharp cracking sound. He hoped like hell it was her skull that had cracked and not his flashlight. She crumpled to the floor in a heap at his feet.

Yates sneered and shoved her clear of the door so he could close it. There was no hope for it now. He'd searched every square inch of the house and not found what he needed. If it was here, it was damn well hidden.

But he realized that he didn't need to get his hands on it. He only needed it destroyed.

Low laughter started in his chest and rose until it spilled out and rumbled through the house. *Destroyed.* He laughed harder. It was too perfect an opportunity to pass up.

And it was her own fault, really. If she hadn't encouraged those brats of hers to stop by the store after school, her boy never would have left his backpack, and she would have been at home where she belonged while the store burned. The inventory printout and disk would have been destroyed, like they should have been. Damn busybody. Saving paperwork that he didn't want saved.

And cutting herself in on his business with the watches.

Oh, yeah. The bitch deserved what was going to happen to her for interfering and taking what was his.

He didn't even need to make it look like an accident. He'd heard the talk through Cousin Harry that McShane and Riley both thought she had set the fire at the store. Then that kid of hers set fire to their own backyard. What was one more fire for this family of arsonists?

"If we're all agreed that he's not going to show," Mary Jo said with frustration, "then why are we waiting out here in the dark freezing our tushes off?"

"Who's freezing whose tush off," Jack grumbled from the backseat. "At least you're up there with the heater."

"Why didn't you tell me you were cold?" With the push of a button she changed the heater setting from Low to High.

"Since you're obviously still mad at me, I didn't think you'd care."

"Who says I'm mad at you?"

"You haven't kissed me."

"In case you hadn't noticed, there hasn't exactly been much opportunity lately."

"What's wrong with now? It's dark, we're alone, and there's a nice moon."

"And I'm up here and you're back there."

"Is that an invitation?"

Beside her on the seat the radio crackled, making Mary Jo jump. "Mary Jo," came Dalton's voice. "Was your mother supposed to come back tonight?"

Mary Jo picked up the unit and pressed the mic button. "No, why?"

"She just pulled into your driveway."

"You can tell that from inside this barn?"

"I've got George Lewis watching your house. He just radioed me."

"Something's wrong." Mary Jo felt it in her

bones. "She shouldn't be here, she should be in Oklahoma. The man's not coming. I'm going home." She put the car in gear and hit the gas, knocking Jack, who'd been leaning forward, back against the seat.

She'd spoken to Jack, or to herself, he wasn't sure which. In any case, she hadn't told Dalton. Rather than argue with her, since it was too late and she was rounding the barn, Jack reached over the seat and grabbed the radio in time to hear Dalton swear.

"Mary Jo?" Dalton demanded. "The package!"

Mary Jo swore and slammed on the brake. Jack nearly went over into the front seat headfirst.

Grumbling to herself about criminals who didn't show up and mothers who didn't listen, she threw the car door open, grabbed the fake package Dalton had given her, and ran to the overturned barrel a dozen yards away by the old corral gate. She stuffed the package under the barrel, then raced back to the car.

Jack pressed the mic button and told Dalton what was going on.

Mary Jo turned onto the highway at the end of the dirt drive and floorboarded it, once more flinging Jack back in his seat.

"You wanna slow it down?" he complained. "You've got no less than three cops on your tail."

"I dare them to stop me for speeding," she

muttered. "Why would Mother bring the kids home without talking to me first?"

Since he had no answers, Jack kept silent for the rest of the short drive into town.

It didn't seem short to Mary Jo, it seemed interminably long. Urgency licked at her every inch of the way. Disaster loomed thick and heavy in the air, but she had no idea the form it would take, only that she felt it hovering.

As she sped down Main to the turnoff toward her house she thought she heard a siren.

In the backseat Jack hissed. "There's a fire."

It was Mary Jo's house. The eerie, flickering glow behind the drapes was unmistakable to Jack. He and Mary Jo were out of the car in an instant, racing for the front door.

"Mother!" Mary Jo cried.

"I'll find her." Jack raced to the front door, felt it. It was warm, but he had no choice. He had to get in there and find Arliss. "Stay back," he warned Mary Jo.

"Shouldn't you wait for the fire truck?" she asked anxiously.

"Your mother and kids are in there. They can't afford to wait."

Mary Jo mashed her lips together. She was being torn in two. She didn't want Jack to endanger himself, but—

But. Her children and mother were in that burning house. Jack was their only chance. Covering her mouth with both hands, she stood back and let him do what he was trained to do.

Smoke gushed out when he opened the door. It surrounded him, gobbled him up until he disappeared. Shaking, terrified, Mary Jo took a deep breath and followed him into hell.

She was blinded by smoke the instant she stepped through the door and nearly deafened by the shrill beep of every smoke alarm in the house. The heat was shocking. She ran into something large and warm. Reaching with her hand, she grasped . . . a leg. A leg dangling in midair. She screamed, and choked on a lungful of smoke.

"Damn you!" Jack grabbed her by the arm, turned her toward the door, and shoved her out. He was right behind her, with an unconscious Arliss draped over his shoulder. "I said stay out."

On the frozen lawn he lay Arliss down and reached to check her pulse. "I found her on the floor just inside the door."

"Mother! Oh, God, is she breathing?"

"She's breathing. Here comes the pumper. Fire Rescue will be right behind them. Stay with her." He jumped to his feet. "I'll get the kids."

"Oh, God." He was going back in there. For her. For Andy and Heather. Back into that blindness, that airless inferno that had once been her home and was now a death waiting to happen. "Oh, God, Jack."

But he didn't hear her. He had already disappeared back inside.

Beneath her hand her mother stirred. "Mama?" Mary Jo cried.

Coughing and choking, Arliss blinked her eyes open. "Mary Jo?" she croaked.

"It's me, Mama. Don't talk. You're safe now."

Arliss saw the tears streaking her daughter's cheeks and heard her call her Mama. Mary Jo hadn't called her that since turning twelve. Except for the night Al was killed. "Mary Jo?"

"Hush. It's all right. Jack's gone back after the kids."

Arliss struggled to make sense of why she was sprawled out on the freezing ground. "Back to Oklahoma? My head hurts. What am I doing outside?"

"You've got a knot. Do you remember what happened?"

Arliss raised a hand to her forehead. "Something hit me. When I walked in the door." Pushing herself up, she looked around. "My ears are ringing."

"That's a siren. The fire engine's on its way."

"Oh my! Mary Jo, your house is on fire!"

"You . . . you don't remember what happened? Jack pulled you out. He's gone back inside for the kids."

"Back in there?" Arliss's eyes widened.

"Mary Jo, the kids aren't in there. They're in Oklahoma."

Mary Jo's heart stopped. Literally stopped in her chest. "Mama . . . they're not in the house? Andy and Heather are not in the house?"

"I didn't bring them back. I knew something was wrong, and when I couldn't reach you by phone—"

"Mama! Are you sure? You're positive Andy and Heather are not in the house?"

"Of course I'm sure."

Mary Jo remembered the night of that first fire, the horrible heat, the terror, the stinging smoke, the suffocating lack of air. She shook with the terrifying memory. Shook with new fear. "Jack! Oh, God, he won't leave until he finds them. He'll kill himself."

Arliss screamed as Mary Jo raced into the burning house.

# TEN

Fire licked at her heels as she held her breath and felt her way to the stairs. That's where Jack would be, upstairs, searching futilely for Andy and Heather.

The heat scorched her skin and seared the inside of her nose. At the top of the stairs she was forced to breathe. All she got for her effort was smoke that gagged, smoke that choked. Smoke that stung her eyes and made them tear. She tried to call Jack's name, but only coughed.

She never imagined smoke could be so thick. She could see nothing. Absolutely nothing.

She could hear nothing beyond the thundering of her own heart in her ears, and the snapping crackle of the flames as they ate at the base of the stairs behind her.

Never mind the stairs. There were windows upstairs. She could get out through one of them.

But where was Jack? How was she going to find him and let him know the kids were safe?

She tried again to call his name and managed a croak before she gagged on smoke. Groping along the wall, she headed for Andy's room. There was the door to her room. Jack wouldn't look there until he decided the kids' rooms were empty. Had he had that much time?

She had a sudden vision of the two of them groping from room to room, always missing each other, until the smoke and flames claimed them. How sad, everyone would say, that their bodies were found only feet apart.

*No!* They were not going to die in this fire. They had only just found each other. Andy and Heather needed them. They needed their mother, and they needed Jack's strong hand and steady influence. She was determined they would have both.

She passed her room and felt her way, coughing and choking, to Andy's room. Surely if Jack were near he could hear her coughing. He must be coughing, too, but she couldn't hear him.

*Jack!*

Thoughts of Andy made her remember again the lessons he'd learned in school. From Jack. About keeping low to avoid the worst of the smoke. She crouched. Was it thinner down here?

Maybe, but not enough to help. She was still

blind, still choking. Her ribs were ready to crack and her throat felt like she'd been gargling ground glass.

*Jack!*

They literally bumped into each other in the hall between Andy and Heather's rooms. She could tell by the way he gripped her that he was shocked to find her there, but he, too, could do little more than cough when he tried to talk.

In truth, Jack was too shocked to talk. What the *hell* was she doing here?

But he would save his questions, and the energy it would take to ask them, until he'd found Andy and Heather and got them all out of this hell.

Over the roar of the flames he finally heard the siren on Pumper Number One. It seemed like hours since he'd reentered the house, but in fact had surely been less than two minutes. If it had been longer than that and the crew was just now getting here, he would have somebody's ass for breakfast.

But the crew would have enough to do without having to rescue their chief. He could lower Mary Jo and the kids out a window. But first he had to find the kids.

"Can't find them," he managed to croak in Mary Jo's ear.

"Safe—not here."

He'd never heard sweeter words. Grabbing

Mary Jo by the arm, he hauled her up and back down the hall to her studio. It was the farthest room from the fire. There he closed the door and propped Mary Jo against the wall. He knocked over at least a half dozen paintings on his way to the window.

When he got the window opened smoke swept through the room and out into the night. He went back for Mary Jo and dragged her to the window. So much smoke was still being sucked beneath the door and outside that they had to lean far out to draw a breath.

Someone out in the yard shouted. "I see them! There they are!"

Jack waved to indicate they were all right.

"The kids aren't here?" He had to be sure he'd understood her correctly.

"No." She shook her head. "Mother left them in Oklahoma."

"Thank God."

Mary Jo could only nod as another coughing fit seized her.

Someone ran over with a ladder and Jack sent Mary Jo down first.

Mary Jo collapsed into the waiting arms of a member of the Fire Rescue squad. Her eyes stung so badly that she couldn't see well enough to tell who it was. She didn't care. She kissed him anyway.

"What the hell?" The man holding her stepped back and looked up at the window.

Neighbors had poured from their houses in night clothes and overcoats, filling their yards, the street. All were looking, pointing up at the window.

Mary Jo looked. There was Jack, hanging out of the window, smoke billowing out around him like an unholy halo while he lowered one of her paintings to a firefighter.

With what was left of her voice Mary Jo shrieked. "You idiot! Forget the damn paintings and get your butt out of there!"

"Ah," someone said behind her. "The voice of true love."

Despite the seriousness of the situation, or perhaps because of it, everyone within earshot of that last comment laughed.

Jack followed the painting out the window and down the ladder and had Mary Jo in his arms before she could blink.

"What in the hell did you think you were doing, coming into a burning house like that?"

He was furious. Livid, if the look in his red-rimmed eyes was anything to go by. Mary Jo gave back as good as she got. "I was saving your hide, that's what."

"I'm an experienced firefighter. I don't need you to take care of me in a fire. You could have been killed."

"You *would* have been, if I hadn't told you the kids weren't there."

"I was doing fine—"

"You would have kept looking for them until you collapsed rather than leave that house thinking you'd left them inside. Admit it."

That shut him up. He couldn't argue with the truth. Jack would not have left the house thinking Andy and Heather were hiding from the fire and he just couldn't find them. Even adults tried to hide from fire, behind beds, closed doors, whatever was handy. Jack had already searched under the bed in Heather's room and in her closet, hoping against hope that his hand would touch that tiny little body and find it still breathing.

The fight went out of him. "You're right. I would have kept looking."

"I love you, Jack Riley."

Jack's chest tightened. "I'm still a firefighter, Mary Jo. I'll always be a firefighter."

"I know."

Jack was afraid, so very much afraid, that it was the heat of the moment speaking. He'd rushed into a burning house to try to save her children. She was grateful. In a day or two the hero worship would fade and she would remember that she didn't want a man with a dangerous job, a man who risked his life for others.

When he didn't say anything, she looked a little hurt. "Is that all you have to say?"

"Marry me."

There was so much noise and confusion

around them while her home was going up in flames and men rushed to save what they could. Mary Jo thought surely she'd heard wrong. "What?"

"You heard me. You say you love me, prove it. Marry me."

"You think I don't mean it?"

"Something like that."

"And you want to marry me anyway?"

He shrugged, feeling more unsure of himself than he ever had. "Maybe I'll grow on you. Maybe you'll get so used to having me around that you'll love me despite what I do for a living."

A huge lump formed in Mary Jo's throat. "Oh, Jack." She placed her hands on his soot-covered face. "I love in you part *because* of what you do."

"But I thought—"

"So did I. I was wrong. I'm proud of what you do. Proud of you. I love you, Jack Riley, just the way you are."

Through the nerves and the residual fear, Jack grinned. "Is that a yes?"

Mary Jo laughed and threw her arms around his neck. "That is definitely a yes."

He kissed her hard and fast, then leaned back in her arms. "There's just one thing, though."

"What's that?"

"If it's all the same to you, I'd just as soon

not come across you inside any more burning buildings."

Mary Jo was just about to answer that it was fine with her when Jack kissed her again. Behind her closed eyelids, she could have sworn she saw a flashbulb go off.

# EPILOGUE

After an exciting winter, the town of Two Oaks settled into spring and things more or less got back to normal. Folks were darn glad of it, too.

Well, there was that one incident at the Baptist Church the first week of June when young Andy Simpson, in his last official act as the man of the family before he gave that title over to his new stepfather, knocked a candle over during his mother's wedding to the local fire chief. That was pretty exciting for a few minutes, the way the draping in front of the altar went up in flames. But since the fire chief was so handy and all, being the groom of the day, things were under control in no time and the rest of the ceremony went off without a hitch.

Nice reception they had, once Arliss Kelley and Mary Riley quit crying over how beautiful their children looked while marrying each other.

Some of Jack's firehouse buddies from Dallas came up for the do. Mary Jo had her share of out-of-town friends, too. Some bigwig general manager of an Oklahoma City television station by the name of Morgan brought his wife, Rachel, who was Mary Jo's good friend. And folks thought it was right fittin' that Mr. and Mrs. Simpson, the parents of the new bride's late husband, came. And that Houston fella, Zane, who'd been Al Simpson's partner with the OSBI. That poor fella's little wife, Becca, had been so pregnant that Houston was afraid to take his eyes off her for a minute.

Yes, sir, that wedding and reception were the highlight of the spring.

These days the topic of conversation was mainly that of arguing over the supposed merits of the stoplight on Main Street, or speculating if the town was ever going to get another jewelry store, what with the previous owner of Two Oaks Gems awaiting trial on arson and various other charges.

That was sure a kicker when the news came out about ol' Bob Yates. Why, his uncle and his granddaddy both were probably turning over in their graves. It seems that Bob liked to bet on the horses over at Ruidoso Downs. Thing was, he wasn't very lucky at it and got himself in deep doodoo with some not very nice fellas. To pay them off he'd called up an old college buddy, who arranged for Bob to be the middleman for some stolen computer chips that were said to be ready to revolutionize the entire computer industry.

Imagine, hiding computer chips inside Rolex watches.

Poor ol' Bob, though, wasn't much luckier at crime than he was at betting on horses. It seems that a customer in the store when the watches arrived overheard that the safe in the back office was broken and wouldn't lock. Being in dire need of money to get himself over a broken heart and a likewise broken bank account, the fella came back after hours and helped himself. Beat Bob to the goods, so to speak. He was still awaiting trial.

And there Bob was, no watches with stolen computer chips to pass along to get the money to pay off his gangster acquaintances. Imagine him thinking that sweet little Mary Jo Simpson, his own trusted employee, had stolen the watches.

Bob's cousin Harry was so busted up over the whole mess that he up and resigned as county sheriff. Bob's wife, Karen, had divorced him right off and moved home to her mama's in Dallas. Swore she could never hold her head up in the town of Two Oaks again.

Over in what used to be called the Simpson house but was now more rightly known as the Riley place, there'd been a few adjustments to be made after Mary Jo and Jack got married. The most obvious one to anyone familiar with Mary

Jo's living room decor was the absence of the three flags on her mantel.

In their place stood four eight-by-ten photographs. The first three were black-and-whites: Jack kissing Mary Jo in front of the burning jewelry store; Jack kissing Mary Jo in her burning backyard; and Jack kissing Mary Jo in front of her burning house. The fourth one was in color: Jack kissing his new bride for the very first time. Nothing was burning in this picture except the candle in Andy Simpson's hands in the foreground.

It was the mischievous, avid look in the boy's eyes as he stared at the flame that had his mother worried.

"Do you think he's going to grow up to be an arsonist?" Mary Jo asked Jack. It was July Fourth, and Andy had taken a more than usual interest in the fireworks the town set off over at the ball park.

Jack pulled his wife of one month closer beneath the sheets and breathed in the scent of her hair. He would never get enough of smelling her, holding her, making love with her. "I thought you were more worried about him wanting to be a cop."

"I should have kept my wishes to myself. A cop's better than a pyromaniac."

Jack laughed. "I don't think you'll have to worry about that. He's going to be a firefighter."

"Our little arsonist?"

"You bet. It's a known fact that eighty percent of all firefighters started fires when they were kids."

"You're kidding." She raised up on one forearm and peered at him in the darkness. "What about you?"

"Not me," he protested.

"I'll ask your mother."

"Well, there was that one incident when the hay in the barn caught on fire."

"But it was an accident, right?"

Jack's white teeth flashed with his grin. "That was my story then, and I'm sticking to it."

"Hmm." She wasn't sure she believed that, but she'd let him off the hook for now. "Did I tell you that Zane called this afternoon?"

"Zane Houston? Al's partner? The guy with that cute wife who came to our wedding?"

"That cute, very pregnant wife who is no longer pregnant."

"She had the baby?"

"A boy, born yesterday. They named him Al."

Jack touched a finger to her cheek and kissed her softly. "I'm glad. Although since he'll never get to meet the man he's named for, the kid may not be too thrilled with a name like Al," he added with a chuckle. "And speaking of kids . . ."

"Were we?"

"You were."

"Meaning?"

"Meaning, are you gonna talk all night?"

Mary Jo shifted in bed, purposely rubbing her leg across his thighs. "You had something else in mind?"

"Not much," he allowed. "I just thought maybe we ought to get started on that third baby you've been wanting."

Mary Jo took in a slow, deep breath. They had talked about having another child, but not since right before the wedding. They'd agreed they wanted one, but had not talked about when. "Have I told you lately that I love you?"

"You have, but I like to hear it, so say it whenever you want. Is that a yes?"

"Oh, yes. It's definitely a yes."

It wasn't until much later that night when Jack spoke again. "I guess I should warn you."

"About what?" Mary Jo asked with a rumble in her voice that sounded amazingly like the purr of a contented cat.

"That my father is a twin."

"Jack! *Now* you tell me?"


Andy and Heather's baby brother and sister were born exactly nine months later.

The twin Riley babies were the talk of the town in Two Oaks, Texas, for the next twenty years.

# THE EDITORS' CORNER

People often ask how we can keep track of all the LOVESWEPTs, the authors and their stories, and good grief, all the characters! It's actually pretty easy. We're fortunate to have some of the most talented authors writing for us, telling beautiful stories about memorable and endearing characters. To lose track of them would be like losing track of what's going on in the lives of our closest friends! The August LOVESWEPT lineup is no exception to the rule. We hope you enjoy these stories as much as we did!

First up is Loveswept favorite Laura Taylor, who leaves us all breathless with **ANTICIPATION**, LOVESWEPT #846. Viva Conrad fled Kentucky without warning, leaving behind a life she adored and silencing her dreams in a gamble to keep the people she loved safe. Spencer Hammond will stop at nothing to discover the truth of her desertion and her involvement in his stepbrother's death. Brought together by the wishes of a dead man and a racehorse guaranteed to win it all, Viva and Spencer must learn to tolerate each other for the good of their investment. As their individual agendas collide, the two must also deal with the unexpected attraction that flares to life between them, amid secrets that threaten to destroy what they long to build together. Suspense rivals sensuality in Laura Taylor's riveting saga of dangerous secrets and shadowy seductions.

Next on the docket, Peggy Webb returns with an exciting romp through the southern part of heaven with a man who can only be referred to as Tarzan on a Harley. After having headed for the hills to forget a thoughtless scoundrel, B. J. Corban is now stuck with the job of **BRINGING UP BAXTER**, LOVE-SWEPT #847. Baxter, you see, is this cute little puppy who's trying to steal everyone's heart (and the limelight as well). However, when B. J. gets a look at the muscular legs encased in the tight leather pants of Crash Beauregard, she scents danger and irresistible possibilities. Prim lawyer that she is, B. J. tries to resist the devilish charms of the sexy rebel. Peggy teases and tempts with delicious wit and delectable humor as she reveals just what happens when a big-city lawyer and a judge from the sticks tangle over a case of true love.

Detective Aaron Stone desperately needs a break in the murder investigation of notorious drug dealer Owen Blake in **BLACK VELVET**, LOVESWEPT #848 by Kristen Robinette. So when a phone call comes through for the deceased dealer, Aaron jumps on this new lead. On a lark, Katherine Jackson tries to contact the man of her dreams, just to see if he really exists. When they meet, the attraction sizzles and Aaron must now decide whether this woman with the face of an angel bears the heart of a killer. Katherine's dreams begin to reveal more secrets, this time involving Aaron. These secrets evoke more emotions than Aaron can bear and it's up to Katherine to give him new hope where none had seemed possible. Kristen Robinette's story is woven of equal parts mesmerizing mystery and heartbreaking emotion and is guaranteed to touch your heart, as a man's heart is slowly healed by the love of his life.

Please welcome newcomer Kathy DiSanto, who gives us a story about a man struggling to decide if women want him **FOR LOVE OR MONEY, LOVESWEPT #849**. Acting on a dare has never worked out well for teacher Jennifer Casey. But when she's *triple-dog* dared to write a letter to millionaire Brent Maddox, her pride leaves her no choice. When he shows up at her doorstep with a dare of his own, Jen must spend a week with Brent in his "natural habitat" to see how the other half lives. Hobnobbing with the rich and famous has taught Jen that their lives are vastly different from hers, but can Brent teach her otherwise? As their tempers collide and their hearts unite, Jen and Brent must build a bridge between their two worlds. Kathy's romantic tale of two unlikely lovers is fast-paced and funny—and one you'll never forget!

By now you guys must have seen the new LOVESWEPT look. We hope you are as pleased with it as we are. Please let us know what you think by writing to us in care of Joy Abella, or even visiting our BDD Online web site (http://www.bdd.com/romance)!

Happy reading!

With warmest regards,

*Shauna Summers*  *Joy Abella*

Shauna Summers          Joy Abella
Editor                  Administrative Editor

P.S. Look for these Bantam women's fiction titles coming in August. From Deborah Smith, one of the freshest voices in romantic fiction, comes **A PLACE TO CALL HOME**, an extraordinary love story begun in childhood friendship and rekindled after twenty years of separation. Bestselling author Jane Feather is back with **THE SILVER ROSE**, the second book in her "Charm Bracelet Trilogy," a tale of two noble families, the legacy of an adulterous passion, and the feud that threatens to spill more blood . . . or bind two hearts against all odds.

Don't miss these extraordinary books
by your favorite Bantam authors!

## On sale in June:

# *TOUCH OF ENCHANTMENT*
### by Teresa Medeiros

# *REMEMBER THE TIME*
### by Annette Reynolds

From the bestselling author of *Breath of Magic* and *Shadows and Lace* comes a beguiling new time-travel love story in the hilarious, magical voice that has made

# Teresa Medeiros

one of the nation's most beloved romance writers.

# *TOUCH OF ENCHANTMENT*

*Heiress Tabitha Lennox considered her paranormal talents a curse, so she dedicated her life to the cold, rational world of science. Until the day she examined the mysterious amulet her mother left her and found herself catapulted seven centuries into the past—directly into the path of a chain-mailed warrior. . . . Sir Colin of Ravenshaw had returned from the Crusades to find his enemy poised to overrun the land where his family had ruled for generations. The last thing he expected was to narrowly avoid trampling a damsel with odd garb and even odder manners. But it is her strange talent that will create trouble beyond Colin's wildest imaginings. For everyone knows that a witch must be burned—and Colin's heart is already aflame. . . .*

He thought the creature was female, but he couldn't be sure. Any hint of its sex was buried beneath a shapeless tunic and a pair of loose leggings. It blinked up at him, its gray eyes startlingly large in its pallid face.

"Who the hell are you?" he growled. "Did that murdering bastard send you to ambush me?"

It lifted its cupped hands a few inches off the ground. "Do I look like someone sent to ambush you?"

The thing had a point. It wore no armor and carried no weapon that he could see, unless you counted those beseeching gray eyes. Definitely female, he decided with a grunt of mingled relief and pain. He might have been too long without a woman, but he'd yet to be swayed by any of the pretty young lads a few of his more jaded comrades favored.

He steadied his grip on the sword, hoping the woman hadn't seen it waver. His chest heaved with exhaustion and he was forced to shake the sweat from his eyes before stealing a desperate glance over his shoulder.

The forest betrayed no sign of pursuit, freeing him to return his attention to his trembling captive. "Have you no answer for my question? Who the hell are you?"

To his surprise, the surly demand ignited a spark of spirit in the wench's eyes. "Wait just a minute! Maybe the question should be, Who the hell are *you*?" Her eyes narrowed in a suspicious glare. "Don't I know you?" She began to mutter beneath her breath as she studied his face, making him wonder if he hadn't snared a lunatic. "Trim the hair. Give him a shave and a bath. Spritz him with Brut and slip him into an off-the-rack suit. Aha!" she crowed. "You're George, aren't you? George . . . George . . . ?" She snapped her fingers. "George Ruggles from Accounting!" She slanted him a glance that was almost coy. "Fess up now, Georgie boy. Did Daddy offer you a raise to play knight in shining armor to my damsel in distress?"

His jaw went slack with shock as she swatted his sword aside and scrambled to her feet, brushing the grass from her shapely rump with both hands. "You can confide in me, you know. I promise it won't affect your Yearly Performance Evaluation."

She was taller than he had expected, taller than any woman of his acquaintance. But far more disconcerting than her height was her brash attitude. Since he'd been old enough to wield a sword, he'd never met anyone, man or woman, who wasn't afraid of him.

The sun was beating down on his head like an anvil. He clenched his teeth against a fresh wave of pain. "You may call me George if it pleases you, my lady, but 'tis *not* my name."

She paced around him, making the horse prance and shy away from her. "Should I call you Prince then? Or will Mr. Charming do? And what would you like to call me? Guenevere perhaps?" She touched a hand to her rumpled hair and batted her sandy eyelashes at him. "Or would you prefer Rapunzel?"

His ears burned beneath her incomprehensible taunts. He could think of several names he'd like to call her, none of them flattering. A small black cat appeared out of nowhere to scamper at her heels, forcing him to rein his stallion in tighter or risk trampling them both. Each nervous shuffle of the horse's hooves jarred his aching bones.

She eyed his cracked leather gauntlets and tarnished chain mail with blatant derision. "So where's your shining armor, Lancelot? Is it back at the condo being polished or did you send it out to the dry cleaners?"

She paced behind him again. All the better to slide a blade between his ribs, he thought dourly. Resisting the urge to clutch his shoulder, he wheeled the horse around to face her. The simple motion made his ears ring and his head spin.

"Cease your infernal pacing, woman!" he bellowed.

"Or I'll—" He hesitated, at a loss to come up with a threat vile enough to stifle this chattering harpy.

She flinched, but the cowed look in her eyes was quickly replaced by defiance. "Or you'll what?" she demanded, resting her hands on her hips. "Carry me off to your castle and ravish me? Chop my saucy little head off?" She shook her head in disgust. "I can't believe Mama thought I'd fall for this chauvinistic crap. Why didn't she just hire a mugger to knock me over the head and steal my purse?"

She marched away from him. Ignoring the warning throb of his muscles, he drove the horse into her path. Before she could change course again, he hefted his sword and nudged aside the fabric of her tunic, bringing the blade's tip to bear against the swell of her left breast. Her eyes widened and she took several hasty steps backward. He urged the stallion forward, pinioning her against the trunk of a slender oak. As her gaze met his, he would have almost sworn he could feel her heart thundering beneath the blade's dangerous caress.

A mixture of fear and doubt flickered through her eyes. "This isn't funny anymore, Mr. Ruggles," she said softly. "I hope you've kept your résumé current, because after I tell my father about this little incident, you'll probably be needing it."

She reached for his blade with a trembling hand, stirring reluctant admiration in him. But when she jerked her hand back, her fingertips were smeared with blood.

At first he feared he had pricked her in his clumsiness. An old shame quickened in his gut, no less keen for its familiarity. He'd striven not to harm any woman since he'd sworn off breaking hearts.

She did not yelp in distress or melt into a swoon. She simply stared at her hand as if seeing it for the first time. "Doesn't feel like ketchup," she muttered, her words even more inexplicable than her actions. She sniffed at her fingers. "Or smell like cherry cough syrup."

She glanced down at her chest. A thin thread of blood trickled between her breasts, affirming his fears. But as her bewildered gaze met his and the ringing in his ears deepened to an inescapable roaring, he realized what she had already discovered. 'Twas not her blood staining her breast, but his own. His blood seeping from his body in welling drops that were rapidly becoming a steady trickle down the blade of his sword. Horror buffeted him as he realized it was he, and not she, who was in danger of swooning. The sword slipped from his numb fingers, tumbling harmlessly to the grass.

He slumped over the horse's neck, clutching at the coarse mane. He could feel his powerful legs weakening, betrayed by the weight of the chain mail that was supposed to protect him. Sweat trickled into his eyes, its relentless sting blinding him.

"Go," he gritted out. "Leave me be."

At first he thought she would obey. He heard her skitter sideways, then hesitate, poised on the brink of flight.

His flesh felt as if it were tearing from his bones as he summoned one last burst of strength to roar, "I bid you to leave my sight, woman. Now!"

The effort shredded the tatters of his will. He could almost feel his pride crumbling along with his resolve, forcing him to choke out the one word he detested above all others. "Please . . ."

Swaying in the saddle, he pried open his eyes to cast her a beseeching glance. Sir Colin of Ravenshaw had never fallen before anyone, especially not a woman.

And in the end he didn't fall before this one either.

He fell on her.

Sometimes the only thing standing in the way of true love is true friendship. . . .

# REMEMBER THE TIME

## by Annette Reynolds

**An emotional, powerful story that celebrates all the joys, fears, and passions of true love.**

*They were the best of friends since high school, an inseparable threesome: Kate Moran, Paul Armstrong, and Mike Fitzgerald. But it was Paul who won Kate's heart and married her, leaving Mike to love Kate from afar. Then, in a tragic accident, Paul died, and for Kate, it was as if she had lost her life, too. Now, after nearly three years of watching Kate mourn, of seeing the girl who loved life become a woman who suffers through it, Mike knows he can't hold back any longer. The time has come to tell her how he feels. And all he can hope is that Kate recognizes what he's known all along: that they've always been perfect for each other. But there are secrets that can shake even the strongest bonds of love and friendship . . . and betrayals that can tear two lovers apart.*

The breeze blowing in from the open window had turned chilly and it woke her. The stiffness in her back brought an involuntary groan, a sound she didn't remember making when she was younger. Like gray hairs and laugh lines that suddenly appeared in her mid-thirties, so these new noises came, too.

The telephone that sat on the end table jangled. It was an old rotary phone from the forties, and she always swore she could see it wiggle and dance as the bell rang. Her cartoon phone. When she picked up, there was no one on the other end. This was a regular occurrence. The C & P Telephone Company—the initials stood for Chesapeake and Potomac but most residents called it Cheapskate and Poky—also seemed to date back to the forties. Kate hung up and waited for it to ring again. And it did.

"Kate? It's Mike. Didn't you see my note?"

"What note?" She could tell by the silence that Mike had closed his eyes in annoyance, and she said, "I heard that."

"I left a note by your front door."

"Where?" she continued to bait him.

"On a pushpin right next to the door. It was on a pink flyer for the SPCA Thrift Shop."

"I guess I didn't realize it was something important. What did it say?"

He picked up on her mood. His voice, a well-moderated blend of East Coast inflection with just a touch of Virginia gentleman, took on a slight Irish lilt. Kate called it his leprechaun voice. "They're havin' their annual half-off sale this weekend."

"What are you talking about?"

She didn't seem to be amused. He must have misjudged her. "Never mind. The gist of the note is that Homer is over here visiting me."

She sighed. "I thought it was a little too quiet."

"He got through that hole in the fence again. I can fix it for you, if you want." There was no reply. "Or not. Do you want me to bring him over?"

"If you must."

"I'm afraid I must. Are you decent?"

She smiled at that. It was a very old joke between them. "Never. Come on over."

Kate was still sitting on the couch when the front door opened four minutes later. She heard Homer's toenails scrabble across the hardwood floor of the entry hall as he raced to the kitchen, and his food bowl. He never understood why it wasn't perpetually full.

Mike's voice reached her. "Kate? Where are you?"

"In here."

"Where?"

"Just follow the sound of my voice."

"My, we're in a good mood," Mike said, entering the den. He took in her rumpled shirt and puffy eyes. Her dark auburn hair, which usually hung in gleaming waves to her shoulders, had been pulled back in a barrette that now stuck out at an angle. Wisps of hair had escaped and formed odd cowlicks. "And you got all dolled up just for me. You really shouldn't have."

"Nice to see you, too." As she spoke the words, her hands went to the barrette and removed it. She ran her fingers through her hair. "I was taking a nap."

Mike leaned against the built-in bookcase and folded his arms across his chest. "Late dinner for two last night?"

Kate eyed him for a split second, then retorted, "Yeah, me and David Letterman."

"Y'know, if you actually went to sleep before two A.M. you wouldn't wake up feeling like crap every day."

"Don't start, Mike. And not that it's any of your business, but I do go to sleep before two A.M."

"Falling asleep on the couch with the TV on isn't what I'd call getting a good night's sleep."

Almost too weary to argue, Kate fixed him with a look that would crumble stone. "I don't need another mother, thanks. And how the hell do you know where I sleep?"

"I got in late last night. Saw the light."

"What is it with you Fitzgeralds? If you're going to lecture me like I'm a child, then you can go home now."

Not wanting to be banished, he unfolded his arms and held them up in surrender. "Hey, I'm sorry. Can we start over?"

Kate looked down at the carpet. "Yeah, sorry. It's been a bad day." Her head came up and she tried to smile. "I could use a cup of coffee. Want one?"

Mike angled his body into one of the kitchen chairs and, with his foot, pulled another chair toward him and propped his long legs on it. Homer, always glad for any company, sat at his side and let Mike scratch his head.

Kate measured coffee into the filter and then took the carafe to the sink. Forgetting the cold water tap was practically welded shut, she grunted when it wouldn't turn. Swearing under her breath, she set the pot down to free both hands. It still wouldn't budge and Mike, hiding a grin, asked, "Can I get that for you?"

"Thanks, but I can do it," she answered, removing the pliers from the drawer.

He shook his head, but didn't say anything.

Once the coffee was perking, Kate realized she still hadn't started the dishwasher. Pulling two mugs out of the top rack, she began washing them.

"Are you sure this isn't too much trouble? We could always go to The Beverley."

Kate turned and gave him a warning look as she dried the mugs with a paper towel. All the dishcloths were in the dryer.

Setting a mug on the table next to him, she asked, "You take milk, right?"

He nodded and watched her open the refrigerator.

She stood in front of it for what seemed a very long time, and Mike suddenly understood why. "Hey, I can drink it black if you're out."

"No!" Her voice wavered momentarily. "No, I must have something you can use."

Mike's legs slipped off the chair and he sat up. "It's okay. Really."

She had closed the door and moved to the cupboards, her hands pushing aside cans and jars. Mike stood as she began frantically pawing through drawers. When her fingers closed around a small packet, she felt triumphant, until she saw it was a Wash'n Dri. Slamming it down on the counter, the tears finally came. Mike's hand on her shoulder made her flinch.

"Stop it, Kate. Forget it."

"I know I'll find something," she said between sobs.

"Katie, darlin', I can't stand to see you like this."

Her voice took on a hard edge. "Then go home, 'cause this is what I am now."

It took all the strength he had not to pull her to him. "I don't think you need to be alone."

"I think I know what I need."

"Christ, but you are pigheaded." He took a deep breath. "Do you really want me to go?" he asked, not wanting to hear her answer.

She nodded. "Yeah—go."

He stared at the back of her head before turning away. He left the way he came. It took her a few moments to realize she'd forgotten to thank him. Picking up one of the two clean mugs, she flung it across the room. It hit the stove top, shattering. Homer slunk out of the room, leaving her alone. It was what she wanted, after all. Wasn't it?

❖―――――❖

He had loved her—no, make that obsessed over her—for as long as he could remember. It was their junior year. She had walked into their English class that first week of October—her family had just moved to the area—and she captured the heart of every male in the room.

The teacher introduces her as Kathleen Moran and asks her to tell the class a little about herself. With a tremendous amount of poise, she walks to the teacher's desk, puts down her purse and books, and says,

"Hi. I just moved here from Oklahoma but I was born in Pennsylvania. My father just retired from the Army and we're in Staunton because he's going to be teaching at the military academy. This is the eighth school I've gone to, but so far it seems like the friendliest." She looks at the faces watching her and notices a familiar one. It is a girl named Chris who lives across the street from her. They have already spoken and so she focuses on her when she says, "I've lived in five states and one foreign country but I've never seen any place as pretty as Staunton. And, by the way, everyone calls me Kate."

Her smile encompasses the entire room. It is impossible not to smile back at her. The boys have seen all they need to know about Kate Moran. Their minds are filled with ideas on how to make this auburn-haired beauty feel welcome. The girls' minds, however, are filled with other, less-than-charitable, ideas. And yet they find themselves smiling at her, too. Chris, Kate's first acquaintance, has already spread the word about this newcomer but nothing has prepared them for what she looks like. Chris's assessment of the situation had been, "You won't like her when you see her, but once you talk to her, she's pretty cool."

The teacher waits for the whispers to subside, then says, "Maybe you can tell us about some of your interests."

Kate has already picked up her belongings from the

teacher's desk and is walking toward an empty desk, when she tosses off, "Oh, I like rock music, reading, antiques. But I love baseball." She carefully slides her miniskirted body into the seat. All male eyes move their field of vision down a foot. "Especially the San Francisco Giants." Kate takes a pencil out of her purse, opens her spiral notebook, and looks up at the teacher expectantly.

"Yes. Well. Thank you, Kate." He has to physically pull himself away from her dark blue eyes. "We're glad to have you here."

Paul Armstrong leans forward and taps Mike on the shoulder. Best friends since the third grade, Mike knows what Paul is going to say before the words are out of his mouth.

"I think I'm in love," Paul whispers. It is his standard remark, made in his usual offhand way. This time he means it.

"You and me both, bud. Think she can handle the Dynamic Duo?" comes Mike's conditioned response. He keeps his voice light, but his heart feels heavy. He really wants this one, but Kate Moran seems to be made for Paul. And they agreed a long time ago not to let a girl get in the way of their friendship.

What did they know at the age of sixteen? They were young and stupid. And in the end it didn't really matter anyway. Kate had come into the lives of Paul and Mike not knowing the rules, and when Paul Armstrong saw her that crisp October day, the rule book got tossed out the window.

Mike held a glass of J & B as he stared out the bay window in his bedroom. With all the leaves off the trees, he had a clear view of her house. The only light he could see came from the den. It seemed to be the only room she used anymore. His sister had told him that she hadn't slept in the bedroom she'd shared with Paul since his death. Kate kept her clothes there and used it as a rather large dressing room, but that was it.

There was a living room and dining room. Both were formal. Packed with antiques that Kate had collected throughout her travels with Paul, they reminded Mike of some of the historic homes he'd visited. Filled with beautiful furnishings, but never used, they seemed like stage settings waiting for the players to make their entrance and bring them to life. Paul and Kate used to give legendary parties. Now, no one entered those rooms.

She had two guest rooms on the second floor. They were at the back of the house, and he guessed she slept in one of them when she wasn't using the couch in the den. Like most Victorian houses, it had one very large bathroom on the second floor, and a very tiny W.C. on the main floor. And, finally, there was the little tower room. He'd been in it only once, when he and Paul had moved some old boxes of papers out of the den. It had been in the dead of winter and they could see their breath as they piled the five years' worth of tax paperwork in a corner. At the time it seemed that the room contained all the usual things people had in their attics . . . Christmas decorations, old clothing that no one wanted, a shelf covered with magazines, and broken things that needed mending that no one ever got around to.

Mike brought the highball glass to his lips and sipped the scotch. The ice had melted. It tasted like warm medicine, and he grimaced. Finishing it in one gulp, he turned from the window and went back downstairs to wait for Sheryl and his nephew, Matt. He hadn't seen the boy in nearly a year and he was looking forward to it. He had wanted to invite Kate over, too. That was, rather apparently, out of the question.

# On sale in July:

*A PLACE TO CALL HOME*
**by Deborah Smith**


*THE SILVER ROSE*
**by Jane Feather**